Donald Fraser

Thomas Chalmers

D.D., LL.D

Donald Fraser

Thomas Chalmers
D.D., LL.D

ISBN/EAN: 9783337398491

Printed in Europe, USA, Canada, Australia, Japan

Cover: Foto ©Andreas Hilbeck / pixelio.de

More available books at **www.hansebooks.com**

THOMAS CHALMERS,

D.D., LL.D.

BY

DONALD FRASER, D.D.

New York:

A. C. ARMSTRONG AND SON,

714 BROADWAY.

MDCCCLXXXII.

PREFACE.

—◦◦◦—

THE Memoirs of Dr. Chalmers by his son-in-law, the Rev. Dr. Hanna, were published in four volumes in the year 1849. A volume of correspondence followed. The work is one of great interest and permanent value for all who wish to know what Chalmers was and to understand the history of his time. We have, as a matter of course, taken it as our chief guide and authority.

A biographical *libellus* on Chalmers by the late Mr. James Dodds is a vigorous eulogium. There is also an excellent and very appreciative sketch of his characteristics in a volume on the Christian Life by Dr. Peter Bayne, published more than twenty years ago. From such sources, with his voluminous writings, and the vivid reminiscences of him which yet survive, there is no lack of materials for our little book. The difficulty rather lies in the arrangement and condensation of them.

CONTENTS

CHAPTER I.

(1730—1803.)

A T East Anstruther, a little seaport on the Frith of
Forth, the greatest Scotsman of modern times was
born. We do not say the greatest genius, or the highest
literary ornament of Scotland; the names of Burns,
Scott, and Carlyle would forbid such an assertion. But
we say, again, the greatest man, the most important and
influential personality that has sprung up in Scotland for
at least two hundred years. As Sir Arthur Helps has
observed, "Greatness is not general dexterity carried to
any extent, nor proficiency in any one subject of human
endeavour." It depends on mental and moral calibre as
a whole. It requires a combination of power to think
and power to do; power to impress and power to impel;
insight and energy, loftiness and firmness, force and
simplicity. And with such tests before our minds, we
call Thomas Chalmers great.

2

His father, John Chalmers, "dyer, shipowner, and general merchant," was a citizen of the old God-fearing type. He was characterised by moral worth and religious steadfastness, rather than by any intellectual property. Mrs. Chalmers seems to have been likeminded, good and devout, but not bright as the mothers of eminent persons so often are, and strangely deficient in the sense of humour. To this worthy couple were born fourteen children, most of whom grew up shrewd, kindly people of their class, but nothing more. The sixth, however, who was born on the 1st March, 1780, was of a larger type and loftier mould — a "son of thunder."

This child, Thomas Chalmers, was not tenderly nourished. His mother had to prepare for the next child, and the next; and so the little boy was committed to the care of a nurse "whose cruelty and deceitfulness haunted his memory through life." To escape from the vixen, he went of his own accord to the parish school at the age of three ! The schoolmasters had no idea of the treasure of mind and heart which lay within that little child, and taught him carelessly. He grew a strong, brave, merry boy—not dull over his books, but heedless. Yet from his earliest years he declared his purpose to become " a minister; " and, as a good many boys have done, he played at preaching to his companions. The text which he chose at the age of six—

" Let brotherly love continue "—showed at all events a kindly nature. It is not alleged that in this juvenile preaching there was any serious meaning or element ; but in those days of old, and, indeed, down to a quite recent period, it was the first thought of a clever Scotch boy in the class of burghers and farmers, and even among those of lower degree, to study for the ministry, or, as some say, for the Church. The pulpit has been and is so great a power in Scotland, and its occupants have been and are so much regarded and discussed among all ranks of its people, that the ambition of youths who wish to influence their generation is very easily turned in that direction before motives more worthy, more spiritual, have begun to work.

The University of St. Andrews was and is the recognised seat of learning and institution of higher education for " the kingdom of Fife." Indeed, at the period to which we refer, it was little more in its " curriculum of Arts " than a school for big boys from the neighbourhood. Examination for entrance there was none. Thomas Chalmers matriculated before he was twelve years of age ; and, as he had shown no precocity at the parish school of Anstruther, and little diligence, his entrance on university classes was premature. The late Lord Campbell, who was a student of St. Andrews at the same period, is said to have been even younger than Chalmers at his matriculation.

Very naturally such boyish students wasted time, and trifled over their books from sheer heedlessness. Certain it is that Thomas Chalmers, ill grounded at the parish school, and much fonder of a roaring game than of study, gave for the first two years of his course at St. Andrews no indication or promise of intellectual ardour. The Latin and Greek classics had no charm for his mind, and this not merely on account of his extreme youth, but also through the defect of the critical and literary faculty in his mind. He never was or could be a *littérateur.* In after years he endeavoured to improve his Latin, New Testament Greek, and Hebrew, as part of his equipment for a Chair of Theology ; but it is to be regretted that through early neglect of classical learning and criticism, he lost a discipline that might have been of great service to him in chastening his style, pruning excrescences, and giving finish and grace to his diction.

In the third winter, however, the mind of the student woke as from sleep. He had entered the class of Mathematics, and what seems to some a cold, hard science had for his brain a charm beyond romance. It suited him well to deal with definite proportions and magnitudes, and to reason on necessary properties, driving up the matter to ultimate and certain conclusions. At once he took a distinguished place among his fellows, and became for his years a remarkable mathematician.

The earlier fancy for the ministry gave place in his mind
to a new ambition to become Professor of Mathematics
in one of the national Universities. It is interesting to
read in connection with this the observations of Lock ·
hart, the biographer of Sir Walter Scott, who heard
Chalmers preach in Glasgow, at the age of thirty-five,
and wrote of him thus in " Peter's Letters to his Kins-
folk " : " It is without exception the most marked
mathematical forehead I ever met with, being far wider
across the eyebrows than either Mr. Playfair's or Mr.
(Sir John) Leslie's, and having the eyebrows themselves
lifted up at their exterior ends, quite out of the usual
line—a peculiarity which Spurzheim had remarked in
the countenances of almost all the great mathematical
or calculating geniuses—such, for example, if I rightly
remember, as Sir Isaac Newton himself, Kaestener, Euler,
and many others."

The intellectual vigour which the mathematics had
evoked was carried forward into other fields of study,
and Chalmers became one of the conspicuous students
of his college. The strong mind once wakened was
never to slumber again. And one of its first wants
was a competent expression of itself through language.
Till now, Chalmers had thought as a child and talked as
a child ; but having begun to think soberly and strongly,
he needed a corresponding utterance. Accordingly, we
find him studying English and the formation of a style ;

and two years sufficed to make a youth who, though a university undergraduate, could scarcely spell or write correctly, master of a diction and a cadence which, however open in some respects to criticism, fitted his emphatic mind and well expressed both his feeling and his thought. Specimens of his later college compositions which his biographer has furnished are written with singular force if not beauty of language, and are interesting as firstfruits of that billowy Chalmerian style, which is as marked as the Johnsonian, and which proved capable of marvellous rhetorical and oratorical effect. It did so at all events as written by Chalmers himself and by the late Henry Melvill, though it may not be recommended for general imitation.

At the end of his four winter sessions in Arts, after the Scottish fashion, our student, though still holding to the mathematical ambition, resolved to take the course prescribed to candidates for the holy ministry—four winter sessions in the divinity hall. Behold him actually enrolled as a divinity student at the age of fifteen ! Yet even then, or in the following year, we read of his studying with ardour such a work as Jonathan Edwards' treatise on Free Will. No clear conception of the gospel of Christ had yet reached his mind, and the religious atmosphere of "the Hall" at St. Andrews was dry and cold. So Chalmers occupied himself mainly with Natural Theology, and with the speculative discussion of such arduous themes as Free Will, Necessity, and Predestination—surely a remarkable proof of intellectual endowment in so young a mind. Little time now for the games which had been far more loved than books—"golf, football, and particularly handball." No time for light reading—the treatise on Free Will threw the boy into "a twelvemonth of Elysium." Such are his own words. The more astonishing this when we recollect that the treatise in question is one of the most dry and severe arguments that has ever been produced. Elysium, indeed! It would more readily suggest to some the gloom of Tartarus. But Chalmers had a sunny spirit. He was capable of deep reverence, but could not be dire or stern ; and so Jonathan Edwards did him good and no harm. As Dr. Bayne has well said, " The mind of Chalmers was of that radically sound and noble order which responds to influences of hope and love rather than those of fear and restraint ; he had an affinity with light."

A singular testimony is borne to the eloquence of this young student in public prayer ! It was then the practice for the theological students at St. Andrews to conduct in rotation daily prayers, morning and evening. All the members of the university were expected to be present, and the prayer hall was thrown open to the public. In his first session Thomas Chalmers was thus required to pray before all—not to read prayers from a book, but to utter a prayer of his own. The prayer which he thus poured out excited such admiration, that " thereafter the people of St. Andrews flocked to the hall when they knew that Chalmers was to pray." Strange boy of sixteen ! More strange burghers of St. Andrews, listening with eager countenances to the boy's studied prayer, consisting chiefly of " eloquent descriptions of the attributes and works of God," as though it were a sermon addressed to them, rather than an appeal to the throne of the Heavenly Grace ! In later years, Thomas Chalmers learned a simpler and more evangelical devotion ; but the prayers he offered publicly in church or class-room were written, and were, in fact, among his most characteristic compositions.

Debating societies there were, almost as a matter of course, among the students, and in one of them Chalmers seems to have spoken often, and shown himself already a formidable intellectual combatant. It was the Theological Society, in which there were two other speakers of much promise, John Campbell, already mentioned, afterwards Lord Chancellor of England, and John Leyden, the Oriental linguist. Leyden was reckoned the best speaker, but when he left the university and tried to preach, he could satisfy neither his audience nor himself, and abandoned the attempt ; whereas Chalmers, as every one knows, became a pulpit prince.

His course accomplished, our student appeared before the Presbytery of St. Andrews to pass the usual examination, and receive "license to preach the gospel." He was still no more than nineteen years of age, and the Presbytery demurred. One of the members, however, urged that he was "a lad o' pregnant pairts;" the plea was admitted, and Thomas Chalmers became an authorised preacher in the Church of Scotland.

But he was by no means eager to preach. As already stated, he had as yet no hold of that gospel which he lived afterwards to proclaim with all his mind and heart. He had indeed the memory of evangelical doctrine as favoured by his own father at Anstruther, who loved the works of Hervey and John Newton, and earnestly commended them to his children on his deathbed; but Thomas, though full of family affection, was little influenced in his opinions by the parental advice. He preferred to follow the prevailing religious tone of the University and Church of St. Andrews, which was non-evangelical, or as the Scottish term is, "Moderate." Accordingly he regarded his "license" by the Presbytery merely as a step of progress in his career. There was as yet no burden of a Divine message on his spirit, which his tongue should make haste to utter.

· His first pulpit appearances, as also his last, were made in England. He preached in the old Scotch church at Wigan, and repeated the sermon at Liverpool on the following Sunday.   His eldest brother, James Chalmers, who was present on those occasions, made thè following report to their father: " It is impossible for me to form an opinion of Thomas as yet ; but the sermon which he gave us in Liverpool, which was the same as we had at Wigan, was in general well liked.   His mode of delivery is expressive, his language beautiful, and his arguments very forcible and strong.   His sermon contained a due mixture of the doctrinal and practical parts of religion, but I think it inclined rather more to the latter.   The subject however required it.   It is the opinion of those who pretend to be judges that he will shine in the pulpit, but as yet he is rather awkward in his appearance.   We, however, are at some pains in adjusting his dress, manner, etc., but he does not seem to pay any great regard to it himself.   His mathematical studies seem to occupy more of his time than the religious."   Grave youths they were —those sons of Scotia—the preacher, nineteen years of age, duly mixing " the doctrinal and practical parts of religion, inclining rather to the latter ; " and the mature critic of twenty-seven, suspending his opinion of his brother, rather hard to please, and not at all so sanguine as " those who pretend to be judges ! "

James did not hide from his father what must have been the unwelcome fact, that Thomas cared more for mathematics than religion.   Even on the journey to Liverpool, and during his stay there, the young preacher was intent on mathematical study, perpetually calculating and demonstrating. Such was at that period the passion of his intellect. On his return to Scotland he actually avoided preaching engagements because they interrupted his studies ; and taking up his residence in Edinburgh, he attended classes in the university of that city, and carried his attainments further than had been possible during his very juvenile course at St. Andrews. Besides his favourite field of Mathematics, he gave himself to Chemistry, Metaphysics, and Ethics.

At this period Chalmers passed through that sceptical conflict of mind which is in some form, and at some time or other, almost inevitable to such intellects. At St. Andrews he had been an admirer of Godwin, who made the tenet of philosophical Necessity a basis of universal doubt, till he became a greater admirer of Jonathan Edwards, who made philosophical Necessity as he taught it, a foundation of faith. But now at Edinburgh came a new peril, in the shape of the *Système de la Nature*, published by the Baron d'Holbach under the pseudonym of M. Mirabaud, an English translation of which was issued in the year 1797. Chalmers was greatly shaken in such Christian belief as he had by the showy materialism of this work, or what he himself afterwards called "its gorgeous generalisations on nature, and truth, and the universe." No doubt his broad and healthy mind would ultimately have found its own way out of any net which the French Materialists of that time could weave; but happily help was at hand in Beattie's essay on Truth, a book now fallen into neglect, and in the prelections of Dr. Robison, the Professor of Natural Philosophy in Edinburgh, also forgotten now, but in his day an efficient and admirable teacher. Our perplexed student was much impressed by a consideration which in after years he was wont to urge with great emphasis on others, viz., the adaptation which exists between the order of nature as observed on the one hand, and the constitution and anticipations of the human mind on the other. This he could not believe to be a result of the fortuitous grouping of material particles.

All through his life Chalmers dealt with the evidences both of Theism and of Christianity, and probably saved many minds from being unhinged in faith by Hume and Voltaire; but, with the exception of the short fight with French Materialism in his youth, to which we have just referred, he seems to have had little personal experience of religious misgiving and doubt. In fact his mind was too realistic for this. It could not play with vague suspense, or bear empty spaces of darkness, but took a large view of all that came within its horizon, then threw itself on plain certainty when that could be had, and when it could not, on broad probability, and was satisfied. He was too wise to say that " Doubt is devil-born," but it was not a thing that haunted him. He had no "spectres of the mind." He was not at all a man to sit brooding over the "Everlasting No," or gazing into the Sibyl cave of Agnosticism. Indeed the scepticism of his age was not so penetrating as that of ours, or the "inward strife" of the time so keen and searching.

Take note here of the fact that Thomas Chalmers had grown up to manhood without vice. His constitution was unhurt by excess, his conduct was free from reproach, and the *mens sana*, just because it dwelt *in corpore sano*, was all the more fitted and likely to find truth and shake off error. He was not without fault. There are indications that he was of a proud, impetuous nature; but he was chaste and sober, honest and true. It was a fine foundation on which to lay an illustrious career.

His mind was now in strong activity; not so much occupied with many books as grappling with great problems, and making its way in a sturdy fashion of its own toward firm conclusions. The most singular circumstance is that the subject which took least hold of his mind was that of which he afterwards became such a distinguished expounder—Divinity. The ambition which still burned within him was to become a university professor, not a preacher of Christ. Altogether a notable masculine character; a thoughtful, high-spirited young man, but with no religious fervour—

Vigorous in health, of hopeful spirits, untouched
By worldly-mindedness or anxious care.

CHAPTER II.

I T is the usage of the Presbyterian Church to license
candidates for the ministry to preach as soon as
they have fulfilled the requisite course of study in Arts
and Divinity, and passed their " trials " before a Presbytery. They are then on public probation for the ministry
of the Word, but are not irrevocably committed to it till
ordained, and not ordained till they obtain or accept a
pastoral charge.

We have seen Mr. Chalmers admitted to this proximate
and probationary position. He did not long continue in
it. He left his studious pursuits in Edinburgh to serve
as " assistant," or curate, in the parish of Cavera, near
Hawick, but held the appointment for only a few months.
The parish of Kilmany needed a pastor ; the patronage
was vested in the senatus of the University of St.
Andrews, and the appointment or presentation was given

to Mr. Chalmers. The truth must be told that its chief attraction in his eyes was the proximity of the parish to the old university town, as permitting him to engage in academical work. And in some small degree his youthful ambition was already gratified, for he was invited to act as assistant to the Professor of Mathematics, and served in that capacity even before his settlement at Kilmany.

On the 12th May, 1803, Thomas Chalmers was ordained with the laying on of the hands of the Presbytery of Cupar. The charge committed to him was a compact rural parish in Fifeshire, occupied by a purely agricultural population. The young minister began his work with a very inadequate sense of its serious character. Intent on academical distinction, he gave to parish duty but a small proportion of his time. His good old father at Anstruther did not like it, and we find the son writing thus to remove the paternal misgivings : " My chief anxiety is to reconcile you to the idea of not confining my whole attention to my ministerial employment. The fact is that no minister finds that necessary. I am able to devote much time and attention to other subjects, and, after all, I discharge my duties, I hope, in a satisfactory manner. Your apprehensions with regard to the dissatisfaction of the parishioners are, I can assure you, quite groundless."

Mr. Chalmers was not invited by the Professor of

Mathematics to continue as assistant during a second winter. It is certain that this did not spring from any discovery of his incompetency. It was believed to originate in jealousy of his superior influence over the class. He felt it keenly; and with the bold and rather combative spirit which went with him through life and would never "knuckle down" to any injustice, he opened extra-academical classes in St. Andrews, and drew the students to his rooms. It was a new and strange thing in the ancient burgh, and if we consider the paucity of students, and the immense influence of the professors in a small university town—an influence which was hostile to the young competitor—the venture was wonderfully successful. The range of Mr. Chalmers' teaching was widened, for he soon added to Mathematics, Chemistry and Geology. The former of these was so congenial to his mind that we find him recurring to it nearly forty years after this, and giving lectures on Chemistry with experiments, and, as he frankly tells us, with "some failures and breakages." The latter science was only in its infancy, and Chalmers was one of the first who had prevision of its value. It is a strong instance of his sagacity that, so early as the year 1804, he feared no injury to Divine revelation from any sure conclusions of Geology. His words to the students were these : "By referring the origin of the globe to a higher antiquity than is assigned to it by the writings of Moses, it has been said that Geology undermines our faith in the inspiration of the Bible, and in all the animating prospects of immortality which it unfolds. This is a false alarm. The writings of Moses do not fix the antiquity of the globe. If they fix anything at all, it is only the antiquity of the species. It is not the interest of Christianity to repress liberty of discussion."

The lectures of the minister of Kilmany attracted notice in all the neighbourhood, and made him a marked man in Fifeshire ; and all the more so as reports went abroad of the independent and even disdainful spirit which he had shown in collision with the professors. One of his brothers writes of him at this period with an uneasy feeling : "I scarcely think he has taken the mode that now leads to preferment, for he flatters no man." A decidedly uncomfortable young man for the university mediocrities at St. Andrews, tricked out in their "little brief authority," and yet in his heart more full than most men are of reverence for real greatness.

Occupied with his classes in St. Andrews, the minister took his cure of souls coolly and leisurely. He preached regularly on Sundays, and paid the visits to his people which were customary, but his heart was not yet given to spiritual work, nor did he know in his own experience the power of the truth, or the cravings of the inward religious life. His very first publication was a pamphlet vindicating the right and competency of the Scottish

clergy to fill university Chairs of Mathematics or
Natural Philosophy, and in course of it he gave expression to sentiments which at a later period, with better
knowledge of ministerial responsibility, he nobly and
publicly retracted. Still they are reproduced to show
what was the attitude of his mind for years after his
ordination. "The author of this pamphlet can assert,
from what to him is the highest of all authority, the
authority of his own experience, that, after the satisfactory discharge of his parish duties, a minister may
enjoy five days in the week of uninterrupted leisure for
the prosecution of any science in which his taste may
dispose him to engage. . . . There is almost no
consumption of intellectual effort in the peculiar employment of a minister. The great doctrines of revelation,
though sublime, are simple. They require no labour of
the midnight oil to understand them ; no parade of
artificial language to impress them upon the hearts of
the people. A minister's duty is the duty of the heart.
It is his to impress the simple and home-bred lessons of
humanity and justice, and the exercises of a sober and
enlightened piety." Thus wrote the accomplished, but
as yet spiritually unenlightened, Chalmers.

And what was this Moderatism which prevailed so
widely at that period in the Church of Scotland, and
laid its cold hand on the minister of Kilmany? It was
the recoil from the fervour of the Covenanter, as in

England high and dry orthodoxy and chill Socinianism showed in two different directions the recoil from the fervour of the Puritan. The only earnestness it ever showed was in repressing earnestness, which it was careful to denounce as fanaticism. It seemed to *ice* even the " milk of the Word ; " and the only honey it could drop was the bland praise of virtue and decorum. It favoured literary taste, but in religion it was a poor frigid thing, and the robust piety of Scotland never accepted or trusted it. The significant fact is that those districts which were most completely and for the longest period surrendered to the influence and teaching of the Moderates, are notoriously those in which certain forms of immorality are most widespread and deeply rooteā. So little can fair words do to make hearts clean ; so little can the praise of virtue effect when Christ and the grace of God are concealed.

The first speech which Mr. Chalmers made in the General Assembly of the Church of Scotland was on no spiritual or exalted theme, but on the Augmentation of Ministerial Stipends. It was not a topic favourable to oratory, but he invested it with an air of freshness which stirred his audience to the inquiry—Who is this ? One heard and marked him who, though in the opposite ecclesiastical camp, resolved not to lose sight of him. It was Dr. Andrew Thomson, of Edinburgh, the vigorous leader, in those days, of the Evangelical party in the Church. At his instance, Chalmers began to write for a magazine called "The Christian Instructor." Then he contributed an article on Christianity to the "Edinburgh Encyclopædia." It was an exposition of the evidences of Christianity rather than of its doctrines; but at all events it indicated that the author's mind was at last turning from his mathematical and chemical pursuits to a more serious consideration of the faith which he was pledged and ordained to teach. He was indeed on the verge of a great inward change.

For the first time in his life he had a serious illness, and was laid aside from public duty for many months. In retirement he reviewed his past years, and was dissatisfied with himself. Then he read books that searched his spirit closely—Pascal's "Pensées," and Wilberforce's "Practical View." The latter, in particular, revealed to him the grave defect of his religion on the fundamental matter of acceptance with God. He saw the insufficiency of his own righteousness, and at first tried to mend it. Most earnestly he fought with himself, endeavouring to suppress all evil inclination, and to rise into a purer and more perfect life. Yet he found himself foiled, and his soul was cast down within him. At length, as God would have it, who had a purpose to fulfil concerning him and concerning many others through him, Thomas Chalmers caught sight of the freeness and simplicity of the gospel of grace, embraced it, and so entered on a peace of conscience and a joy of faith unknown to him till then. In a letter to his youngest brother, within ten years later, he gives the following account of this critical part of his life : " The effect of a very long confinement upon myself was to inspire me with a set of very strenuous resolutions, under which I wrote a journal, and made many a laborious effort to elevate my practice to the standard of the Divine requirements. During this course, however, I got little satisfaction, and felt no repose. I remember that somewhere about the year 1811 I had Wilberforce's ' View ' put into my hands, and, as I got on in reading it, felt myself on the eve of a great revolution in all my opinions about Chris-tianity. I am now most thoroughly of opinion, and it is an opinion founded on experience, that on the system of Do this and live, no peace, and even no true and worthy obedience, can ever be attained. It is—Believe in the Lord Jesus Christ, and thou shalt be saved. When this belief enters the heart, joy and confidence enter along with it. The righteousness which by faith we put on, secures our acceptance with God, and our interest in His promises, and gives us a part in those sanctifying influences by which we are enabled to do with aid from on high what we never can do without it." This is exactly what we find expressed in hi private journal when the new light which had visited his spirit was fresh :

"*Jan.* 7. A review of this day sends home to my conviction the futility of resting a man's hope of salvation on mere obedience; that there is no confidence but in Christ; that the best security, in fact, for the performance of our duties is that faith which works by love, and which, under the blessing of God, will carry us to a height of moral excellence that a mere principle of duty, checked and disappointed as it must often be in its efforts after an unattainable perfection, could never have reached."

Thus the minister of Kilmany became a new man. While his heart was comforted, his seriousness of purpose was deepened, and the inadequate conception of ministerial duty which he had formed and stoutly maintained entirely gave way before the strong convictions which now possessed his soul. We come on such entries in his journal as the following:

"*Feb.* 22. Have begun to read Scott's 'Force of Truth,' and I pray God to beget in me a lively acquiescence in the truth as it is in Jesus."

"*March* 15. Called on sick people in the village. I am a good deal weaned from the ardour for scientific pursuits; and let me direct my undivided attention to theology."

"*April* 23. I am sensible of a growing acquiescence in the peculiar doctrines of the gospel as a scheme of reconciliation for sinners."

"*Aug.* 4. Let me give my whole strength to the conversion and edification of my people."

"*Dec.* 26. Had a call in the evening from A. Paterson, who had been reading 'Baxter on Conversion,' and is much impressed by it. Delighted to hear that it has also been read with impression by others. A. P. finds that he cannot obtain a clear view of Christ. O God, may I grow in experience and capacity for the management of these cases! It is altogether a new field to me, but I hope that my observations will give stability to my views and principles on this subject, and that my senses will be exercised to discern between good and evil."

The parish soon began to feel the change which had passed upon the minister. He had from the first been esteemed by his people for his kindness, and admired in a half-bewildered fashion for the impetuous eloquence with which he urged on them virtues great and small, and for the philippics which, falling in with the great *scare* of the period, he had pronounced against "Bonaparte" in the pulpit. But now an unction appeared in his bearing and his words unknown before. He could not be more impetuous than before, for such was his temperament, but the theme of his ardent speech was not so much the praise of human virtue, or the denunciation of fanaticism, or the rousing of patriotic resistance to Bonaparte, as the commendation of Jesus Christ, and the exposition of a free salvation in Him from all sin.

And now, for the first time, such fruit as the Christian ministry ought to yield began to appear. Inquirers after Christ and after peace with God consulted the minister as no one had consulted him before, and the very morality which he had supposed to be weakened by evangelical preaching was powerfully promoted. The testimony to this which Chalmers bore in his parting address to the parishioners of Kilmany has often been quoted, and it certainly deserves the careful consideration of all who would know how to handle religious truth so as to promote righteousness of life. "I cannot but record the effect of an actual though undesigned experiment which I prosecuted for upwards of twelve years among you. For the greater part of that time I could expatiate on the manners of dishonesty, on the villainy of falsehood, on the despicable arts of calumny; in a word, upon all those deformities of character which awake the natural indignation of the human heart against the pests and the disturbers of human society. It never occurred to me that all this might have been done, and yet every soul of every hearer might have remained in full alienation from God. . . . But the interesting fact is, that during the whole of that period in which I made no attempt against the natural enmity of the mind to God, I certainly did press the reformations of honour and truth and integrity among my people, but I never once heard of any such reformations having been effected amongst them. I am not sensible that all the vehemence with which I urged the virtues and the proprieties of social life had the weight of a feather on the moral habits of my parishioners. And it was not till I got impressed by the utter alienation of the heart in all its desires and affections from God ; it was not till reconciliation to Him became the distinct and the prominent object of my ministerial exertions ; it was not till the free offer of forgiveness through the blood of Christ was urged upon their acceptance, and the Holy Spirit given through the channel of Christ's mediation to all who ask Him was set before them as the unceasing object of their dependence and their prayers, that I ever heard of any of those subordinate reformations which I aforetime made the earnest and the zealous, but, I am afraid, at the same time, the ultimate object of my earlier ministrations. You have taught me that to preach Christ is the only effective way of preaching morality in all its branches ; and out of your humble cottages have I gathered a lesson which I pray God that I may be enabled to carry, with all its simplicity, into a wider theatre."

At this great juncture of his life the sinewy strength of character which was in Chalmers served him well. Becoming an evangelical believer, he became so with his whole heart, and preached accordingly. But he did not rush into any extravagance. When he discovered the weakness of mere moral discourses he did not go over to

Antinomianism, or for a moment lose sight of the interests of goodness and righteousness. It was the power of the gospel to produce such fruits that gave confirmation to the evangelical faith in a mind so practical as his.

He now followed paths of religious reading which he had been wont to avoid. He read and relished such authors as Baxter and Doddridge; above all, he read the Bible much more carefully. And in his private journal he poured out breathings after God, and longings for more faithful testimony to Christ, such as would formerly have seemed to him to be morbid or fanatical, *e.g.:*

"*April* 22 (1812). I am hesitating about my sermon for Dundee. My frequent cogitations about the Dundee exhibition argue, I am afraid, a devotion to the praise of man. Force me wholly into Thyself, O God!"

"*Sunday*, *May* 3. Is it right to fatigue myself thus, or soar so selfishly and ostentatiously above the capacities of my people? O God, may I make a principle of this; and preach not myself, but Christ Jesus my Lord!"

"*May* 6 (From home). Was not vigorous for devotion in the evening. N.B.—When there is no time or opportunity in inns, I can set myself to the great business of intercourse with heaven on the road."

"*May* 10 (at Fettercairn). It is most difficult to maintain a savour of Christianity with the people I am amongst. Let me love Thy people, O God, and court their society!"

" *October* 15. Dined with the Presbytery. Was guilty of several fits of impatience, and feel my weakness. O God, may I take a firm hold of the Saviour, that He may strengthen me to do all things ! Give me the charity that endureth, and banish from my heart suspicion and anger."

The minister of Kilmany was now quite out of harmony with most of the neighbouring ministers, who had passed through no such process of illumination as he had experienced. He was zealous in support of the Bible Society, and they were quite lukewarm. He was full of sympathy and admiration for the Missionary Societies, and they regarded them with a good deal of the dislike and contempt which Sydney Smith poured out in the " Edinburgh Review" on Carey and his coadjutors, as "a nest of consecrated cobblers." The moderate ministers of Fifeshire and Forfarshire regarded Chalmers as having gone mad, an absurd imputation which men of dry and unsympathetic minds often repeated at stages of his subsequent career, which they could not appreciate. But the people began to hold him in just repute, and wherever he now preached, flocked to hear him. In the journal, we find the most naïve avowals of the pleasure experienced in this publicity and popularity with honest struggles against an overweening desire of human applause ; *e.g. :*

" *Jan.* 15 (1813). Extinguish my love of praise, O

God ; and now that my name is afloat on the public, let me cultivate an indifference to human applause."

"*Jan.* 26. Called on Dr. Brown, who gives a high testimony to my article on Christianity. O God, let me not be seduced by the love of praise!"

"*March* 11. Mr. Brewster spent the evening, and I had some conversation with him about my sermon. I fear that this sinful love of distinction still hangs about me. O my God, forgive and cleanse! Let me be fearfully vigilant over this and every other part of my conduct. Let me make a point of bringing forward nothing in conversation for the purpose of signalising myself."

"*Sunday, July* 11. Preached as usual. Miss Collins expressed her satisfaction, and gave me the testimony of another to the good that I had done. I have to record that I felt sweetened and drawn to Miss Collins by this. O my God, search me ; root out all that is sinful in the love of praise!"

The Manse of Kilmany was for many years a bachelor's hall. Mr. Chalmers had one of his sisters to preside over his small household ; but she married, and he was quite alone. He had declared to his friends his resolution not to marry. He thought that his stipend would not suffice for married life, and that by remaining a bachelor he might " live easily, indulge in a good many literary expenses, and command an occasional jaunt to

London." But such vows are broken even by the most resolute men; and Chalmers married in 1812 Grace Pratt, second daughter of Captain Pratt, of the 1st Royals, who was on a visit to an uncle in the parish of Kilmany. It was a union of real affection, and greatly conduced to the comfort and happiness of the busy preacher and pastor. He writes after the marriage to his favourite sister, describing his new domestic experience, and commending his bride in the following characteristic fashion : " It gives me the greatest pleasure to inform you that in my new connection I have found a coadjutor who holds up her face for all the proprieties of a clergyman's family." But though he called her a connection and a coadjutor, he tenderly loved his young wife. The entry in his journal is beautiful :

" *Aug.* 12. Peace, harmony, and affection reign in my abode."

In Kilmany, and afterwards in Glasgow, Chalmers was much given to hospitality, and his journal tells of a constant stream of visitors. One of the most remarkable of those who came under his roof at Kilmany was the English Baptist, whom he very properly characterises as "the judicious Andrew Fuller, able champion and expounder of our common Christianity." The visit of Mr. Fuller to Scotland was in the interest of the Baptist Missions which, at their inception, owed so much to his help and counsel. Never was he more judicious than in the estimate he formed of the minister of Kilmany. A few weeks after his return to his home at Kettering, he wrote: "I saw in my dear friend Chalmers a mind susceptible of strong impressions, a capacity of communicating them to others, a thirst for knowledge, an openness to conviction, and a zeal for the promotion of the kingdom of Christ." Mr. Fuller, however, was scarcely so judicious in urging his new friend to preach extempore. "If that man," said he, "would but throw away his papers in the pulpit, he might be King of Scotland." Chalmers made the experiment, but after a few weeks abandoned it as a comparative failure. Not that he ever was at a loss for language, but his mind was too full and vehement to manage a discourse and keep its parts in due proportion without the use of manuscript. With his usual *naïveté*, he records his experience of extemporaneous preaching.

"*Sunday, Aug.* 15. Felt discouraged, and did not acquit myself to my satisfaction. This want of freedom prevented even a complete and edifying view of the subject. Let me henceforth carry a prepared sermon with me. There is a rapidity and impatience in all my processes. O God, give me to be more calm and judicious!"

All through his life, Chalmers wrote out speeches with care, and committed them to memory, while at the same time he had, as indeed most men have who pursue this course, abundant power of extemporisation on an emergency. Sometimes, as we have ourselves heard him, he spoke the main part of his statement, and then read his peroration with astonishing force. In the pulpit he gained all his great triumphs by preaching from manuscript. It may not be the best method for preachers in general. It is often tame and ineffective; but in the hands of Chalmers, aided by the glow of his countenance, the sweep of his arm, and the stirring power of his voice, it held his audience entranced. "Yon was *fell* reading," observed a good old woman who hated the reading of sermons, but was compelled to make an exception in favour of Chalmers.

There is indeed a popular fallacy about extempore preaching. In the sense of improvisation it is a thing almost unknown among us. Every one whom men care to hear prepares his sermon, though one writes it only in part, another writes in full; and, again, one takes his notes to the pulpit, another his complete manuscript, a third nothing, but trusts to memory. Fuller did not wish Chalmers to improvise. He did not do so himself. The substance and arrangement of his discourses were carefully premeditated and written, though he preached without any notes. He did not write elaborately except for special occasions. In his "Thoughts on Preaching" we find this counsel given to a young minister : "In general I do not think a minister of Jesus Christ should aim at fine composition for the pulpit. We ought to use sound speech and good sense; but if we aspire after great elegance of expression, or become very exact in the formation of our periods, though we may amuse and please the ears of a few, we shall not profit the many, and consequently shall not answer the great end of our ministry. . . . Do not overload your memory with words. . . . Never carry what you write into the pulpit."

Probably the great Baptist preacher of the present day follows the lines of Andrew Fuller, premeditating the matter and structure of the sermon, but only writing partially, always studying simplicity, and never laying manuscript on the desk.   One who is so great a master of the art as Mr. Spurgeon may and will on this plan succeed with any audience; but preachers who have to address many educated people, and who have not the faculty of picking out the best words on the spur of the moment, will generally find it expedient, if not necessary, to write out with care the discourses they mean to deliver. As to the public delivery, it may be from the manuscript unseen but remembered, or from the manuscript laid on the desk.   Mr. Jay practised the former manner; so did Dr. Guthrie, who spoke entirely from remembered manuscript, though with charming ease.   Such memorised preaching has been and is frequent in Scotland, and also abroad, in Roman Catholic, Lutheran, and Reformed pulpits.   It has great advantage for holding the eyes and ears of a congregation, and in the hands of a skilful speaker who does not " talk like a book," it has almost the effect of impromptu ; but it is no more extemporaneous than was the " fell reading " of Jonathan Edwards, Chalmers, Melvill, or Candlish, or is now the " fell reading " of Caird or Liddon.

There is not much more to tell of the ministry at Kilmany. No time now for classes at St. Andrews. The minister glowed with religious earnestness, and watched for souls as one that knew he had to give an account to the Lord at His appearing. He preached not only with more fulness of truth, but with more care than ever— nobly labouring to reduce his rolling periods so as to be more intelligible and useful to the rustics. He stirred up his own parish, and indeed all the neighbourhood, to contribute to the Bible Society, and to the Baptist and Moravian Missions abroad, as the missionary impulse had not yet fallen on the Church of Scotland. Yet he did not abandon his early interest in scientific pursuits. He followed with eagerness the discoveries of Cuvier, and hailed the progress of Geology with a largeness of hope rare among the clergy of his generation.

Thomas Chalmers was now a name in the country. It had come to be widely recognised that a man of rare power and devotedness was rusticating in a small parish of Fifeshire ; and it was inevitable that he should be invited to fill a wider and more conspicuous sphere.

4

CHAPTER III.

(A.D. 1815—1823.)

THE Tron parish of Glasgow was without a minister, and the appointment lay in the gift of the Town Council. Owing to the rivalry of ecclesiastical parties in Scotland at the time, the selection to be made by so public a body for so public a post was watched with keen interest ; and the Town Councillors were well plied with letters of advice. The result was the choice of Mr. Chalmers, of Kilmany, by a decisive majority. He had not sought this promotion ; but when it was offered to him in such a manner, he could not hesitate to accept it, though it was with a sore wrench of feeling that he left the parish to which he had become, especially during the recent years of earnest and successful ministry, affectionately attached, and in which he was greatly beloved. It was in the year 1815, and Chalmers was in early prime, just thirty-five. Glasgow was then a city of 100,000 people, and rapidly growing both in population and in wealth. It was to be the home of Chalmers for eight well-spent years, and for many years thereafter to retain an impress of his energetic spirit.

At once a torrent of popularity broke upon him. The Scotch are a sermon-loving people, and one who could preach as Chalmers did was sure to be in all men's mouths. The dense and eager congregations which gathered before his pulpit gave a constant stimulus to his powers; and, preaching as he now did under a weighty conviction of the responsibilities connected with the sacred function, the minister of the Tron Church surpassed the highest expectations of those who had called him to the great city of the West. Not only was the crowd with him, but good critics, who failed not to remark on his uncouth gestures and barbarous Fifeshire accent, ascribed to him a commanding and glorious eloquence. We have already cited Mr. Lockhart's description of his forehead as that of a mathematician. In his sketch he enters into such minute details as enable us to set before our eyes Chalmers in the pulpit at the age of thirty-five: of middle stature and solid figure, with pale countenance, square cheeks, strong, crisp dark hair, pensive lips, and yet a vigorous mouth, eyelids half closed, and light-coloured, dreamy eyes, that gave forth "flame and fervour" when he warmed into enthusiasm; a noble head, its broad brows surmounted by "an arch

of imagination, while over this again there is a grand apex of high and solemn veneration and love, such as might have graced the bust of Plato." As to the sermon, Lockhart says, " At first there is nothing to make one suspect what riches are in store. He commences in a low and drawling key, which has not even the merit of being solemn, and advances from sentence to sentence, and paragraph to paragraph, while you seek in vain to catch a single echo that gives promise of that which is to come. But, then, with what tenfold richness does this dim preliminary curtain make the glories of his eloquence to shine forth, when the heated spirit at length shakes from it its chill, confining fetters, and bursts out elate and rejoicing in the full splendour of its disimprisoned wings !
. . . I have heard many men deliver sermons far better arranged in regard to argument, and have heard very many deliver sermons far more uniform in elegance both of conception and style ; but, most unquestionably, I have never heard, either in England or Scotland, or in any other country, any preacher whose eloquence is capable of producing an effect so strong and irresistible as his."

A few months after his settlement in Glasgow, the Rev. Thomas Chalmers received from the university of that city the degree of Doctor of Divinity. It is the usage of the Scottish Universities to confer this degree *honoris causa* on such as are deemed by the Senatus to have shown themselves worthy. The professors at St. Andrews probably had not yet quite forgiven the young minister's audacity in teaching rival classes at their doors ; and so they missed the opportunity of enrolling one of the most distinguished men who ever passed through the university among their graduates in Divinity. Henceforward we speak of Dr. Chalmers.

The principal courses of sermons preached by him in Glasgow were published, with the effect of greatly enhancing and extending his reputation. The first series were that of the "Astronomical Discourses," which ran through nine editions in one year. There was a charm of novelty in evangelical eloquence united to a skilled acquaintance with one of the loftiest sciences ; though the objection which was chiefly combated may have occurred to few of his hearers or readers till the preacher suggested it. It was to the effect that the magnitude of the universe as disclosed through the telescope makes the gospel improbable, because it is not reasonable to suppose that the Son of God should intervene in a way so extraordinary as the gospel affirms in behalf of the inhabitants of our planet, a most inconsiderable item in the innumerable multitude of worlds that form His visible creation.

The "Astronomical Discourses" are now little read, but when they were preached on Thursday mornings in Glasgow, busy merchants left their counting-houses, and people of all classes sat or stood breathless under the spell of the orator; and when they issued from the press, men like Canning and Sir James Mackintosh pronounced them magnificent. Undoubtedly it was the popularity of these discourses that first obtained for their author recognition in the literary world. Dr. Chalmers, however, agreed in his old age with John Foster's strictures upon them. His biographer says that " he had quite the feeling towards these discourses that they were a juvenile production with too rich an exuberance of phraseology, to which the pruning knife might beneficially have been applied. Even among his sermons he did not think that they stood first, his 'Commercial Sermons' being always regarded by him as in every respect superior to them." The full title of the second series referred to is "Sermons on the Application of Christianity to the Commercial and Ordinary Affairs of Life." The public did not show the same admiration for them as for the " Astronomical Discourses." The theme gave less scope for lofty and eloquent writing; but we venture to hold that the author's estimate was correct, and that the second was the more valuable series of the two.

Dr. Chalmers in Glasgow was more than a preacher; he was a parish minister, and bent himself most seriously to the duty of his office. Being intent on visiting his parishioners, who numbered about 12,000 souls, he stoutly objected to have his time frittered away in signing papers and performing routine work. He had been exempt from such teasing interruptions at Kilmany, and indeed he never got quite over a certain rusticity and love of *otium cum dignitate.* It must be acknowledged that the demands of the " Glasgow folk " were rather exorbitant. After he had spent three months in the city, Dr. Chalmers wrote to a friend : "This, sir, is a wonderful place; and I am half entertained and half provoked by some of the peculiarities of its people. The peculiarity which bears hardest on me is the incessant demand they have upon all occasions for the personal attendance of the ministers. They must have four to every funeral, or they do not think that it has been genteelly gone through. They must have one or more to all the committees of all the societies. They must fall in at every procession. They must attend examinations innumerable, and eat of the dinners consequent upon these examinations. They have a niche assigned them in almost every public doing, and that niche must be filled up by them, or the doing loses all its solemnity in the eyes of the public. There seems to be a superstitious charm in the very sight of them, and such is the manifold officiality with which they are covered that they must be paraded among all the meetings and all the institutions. . . . I am gradually separating myself from all this trash."

This impatience of unreasonable demands on time

and personal attention came not of indolence, but, as we have said, of an intense desire to fulfil the higher duties of a parish minister. Dr. Chalmers was warmly attached to the old parochial system of Scotland, and had nothing more at heart than to see it worked more thoroughly in town as well as country, for the social as well as the spiritual good of the people. Especially was he anxious to prove its capacity for relieving the wants and elevating the condition of the poor.

Now what he saw in Glasgow was an utter failure to carry out the parochial system for such ends. The people at large were not visited either by ministers or elders, and the poor were relieved in a most unsatisfactory and wasteful manner by funds assessed on the parishes, and dispensed by two public bodies, the General Session and the Town Hospital. The general Poor Law for Scotland had then no existence, but Dr. Chalmers dreaded the introduction of such a measure, and looked on the English Poor Law as an evil omen for his country. Accordingly he set himself firmly to show how a city parish might be worked, and might care for its own poor more economically and, at the same time, with far better moral effect on the population than could ever be obtained on the dry legal system of assessment and stated allowance. For this purpose he actually dissociated himself from the Tron parish and took charge of a new parish called St. John's. The Town Council assigned it to him with *carte blanche* to work it in his own way, and make provision for all the poor within its confines, with exemption from the general assessment. In this new sphere Dr. Chalmers gathered round him not only a zealous eldership, but a powerful band of visitors, whom he "inoculated" (a favourite phrase of his) with his own ideas and enthusiasm. Himself working at their head, and superintending their activity in the districts which he allotted to them, he explored his parish with a mathematical precision as well as a Christian ardour. Within the parochial limits were found 2,161 families, of whom 845 had no seats in any place of worship. To each visitor were assigned about 50 families, and the relief of the poor was dealt with as follows: "We constructed a manual or brief directory, which we put into the hands of the deacons. It laid down the procedure which should be observed on every application that was made for relief. It was our perfect determination that every applicant of ours should be at least as well off as he would have been in any other parish of Glasgow, *had his circumstances there been as well known ;* so that, surrounded though we were by hostile and vigilant observers, no case of scandalous allowance, or still less of scandalous neglect, was ever made out against us. The only distinction between us and our neighbours lay in this, that these circumstances were by us most thoroughly scrutinised, and that with the view of being thoroughly ascertained, and that very generally, in the progress of the investigation, we came in sight of opportunities or openings for some one or other of those preventive expedients by which any act of public charity was made all the less necessary, or very often superseded altogether."

Nothing Utopian in this. A most sober-minded, rational, and minutely systematic plan. It gave far more security against imposture than any Charity Organization Committee can furnish, while it avoided the detective aspect, and spread through the dwellings of the poor a warm breath of Christian helpfulness and love. The results were admirable. To the parishioners of St. John's was secured a preferential right to the sittings in the new church, and they so filled them that strangers had difficulty in finding a vacant corner. The whole community felt the quickening influence of the systematic, kindly Christian agency by which it was now pervaded. And the poor were well relieved at a cost far below that which was imposed on the surrounding parishes. It is on record that in St. John's, under Dr. Chalmers, the average expense of poor relief was £30 per 1,000 of the population, while in the other parishes of Glasgow it was £200, and in many parishes of England it was at that period, under a Poor Law, £1,000 per 1,000 of the population.

It is surprising that with such proved results the example was not followed throughout all the city; but the system of Chalmers really required a combination of Christian enthusiasm and persistence which probably was not to be found in sufficient strength in any parish but his own. It lasted in St. John's for eighteen years, fourteen of them after Dr. Chalmers had left Glasgow. But one parish could not permanently withstand the general practice of a community which so rapidly outgrew all the old parochial machinery; and when at last the whole relations of the parish ministers to the population of Scotland, both urban and rural, was altered by the events of the year 1843, there was a complete breakdown of the arrangements for the kindly local relief of indigence; and to the great chagrin of Dr. Chalmers, a Poor Law for Scotland was enacted in 1845. But nothing could change his opinion on the general question, and he has left it to us in these words : " It remains an article in our creed that for the relief of general indigence the charity of law ought, in every instance, to be displaced to make room for the charity of principle and of spontaneous kindness."

Every one sees that on the system which Chalmers so stoutly maintained, avaricious and cold-hearted persons, well able to contribute to the relief of distress, might and would evade the call to contribute, or give far less than their due proportion; and that a Poor Law places the burden more evenly on all the citizens— the generous and the selfish, the just and the unjust.

But, on the other hand, it becomes more apparent, year after year, that the administration of a Poor Law, involving the admission of a statutory right to public relief, conduces to improvidence and the weakening of family affection among those who are in humble circumstances, tends to keep down wages unduly in rural districts, discourages the honourable pride of independence, and engenders the pauperism which it relieves. English clergymen of experience at recent Church Congresses, and intelligent philanthropists on every side, more and more keenly deplore those degrading influences of Poor Law administration of which Chalmers warned the country half a century ago.

It was while he was minister of the Tron Church of Glasgow that Dr. Chalmers first found himself famous in London. He had paid a visit of curiosity to the metropolis at an earlier period; but in the year 1817 he proceeded thither, on the invitation of the London Missionary Society, to preach the annual sermon in behalf of that institution. In those days there was no express train in which to rush up from Scotland to London in a night; and Dr. Chalmers, with Mrs. Chalmers and " Mr. Smith, his publisher," spent a month on the leisurely journey. On the way, he made a point of seeing and conversing with James Montgomery, at Sheffield, and Robert Hall, at Leicester. And it may here be remarked that Chalmers, while reserved as to his inward thought and life, was of a healthy, sociable nature. He received many visitors. No doubt he often complained of interruption by "calls" made upon him, and it was inevitable that commonplace people would plague him with the kindest intentions. But he had to take the visitors as they came, and a shrewd man can extract something even out of commonplace people. Men of intellectual and moral eminence passing through Glasgow made a point of calling upon him. For example, in the course of a few days in the summer of 1818, his journal notes the visits of Professor Pictet of Geneva, Rev. Legh Richmond, Mr. Cunningham of Lainshaw (the writer on Prophecy), Lord and Lady Elgin, and Dr. Thomas Brown (the Professor of Moral Philosophy in the University of Edinburgh). The social and friendly nature of Chalmers was also shown by him when from home. Busy man though he was, he knew how to unbend the bow; and, all through his life, found time for seasons of relaxation and travel, and for visiting the homes of his friends.

The missionary sermon was delivered in Surrey Chapel, and it is related that Rowland Hill, the minister, stood during the whole time—an hour and a half—at the foot of the pulpit, " gazing on the preacher with great earnestness, and whenever any sentiment was uttered which met his approval, signifying his assent by a gentle nod of the head and an expressive smile.

Staying for a fortnight in London at this time, and preaching in the small Scots churches in London Wall and Swallow Street—both now extinct—Dr. Chalmers drew to his auditory some of the most eminent men of the day—as Canning, Huskinson, Wilberforce, and Sir James Mackintosh. Canning, though at first quite disappointed, as the hard Fifeshire accent broke upon his ear, was soon arrested, and at the end of the service remarked, "The tartan beats us all." A good phrase; though, of course, Chalmers, as a Lowlander, had no more to do with "the tartan" than any Englishman in the crowd.

After the London manner, attentions and invitations were heaped on the now famous man; but he fled from the "insufferable urgency," and made his way to the Isle of Wight, thence to Bath, where he made acquaintance with Mrs. Hannah More and John Foster—the latter of whom he greatly admired. Thence to Bristol, and through Wales to Liverpool. In a letter to one of his sisters he writes: "We spent three days in Liverpool. I was greatly delighted with the Gladstones, to whom I got an introduction." So the good man returned, unspoilt by all the tide of distinction which had everywhere attended him, back to the parish again—to its urgencies and agencies, the oppressive crowd in public, and the steady pastoral visitation in the dense alleys and squalid closes of Glasgow.

In St. John's parish, the assistant-minister, or curate, for a time, was the afterwards celebrated Edward Irving. Chalmers and he harmonised well, each having a genuine admiration of the other, though there was a practical shrewdness in Chalmers which Irving could not appreciate; and an "over soul" and high pitch of mind in Irving which Chalmers thought *uncanny*. Mr. Irving was not yet generally popular. "His preaching," said Dr. Chalmers, "is like Italian music, appreciated only by connoisseurs."

The assistant went to London, where for a few years he made a great sensation. His successor was Mr. Smyth, afterwards Dr. Smyth, and minister, first of the parish, and then of the Free Church of St. John's—a far less striking man than Irving, but safer, and more suited to the post. From his pen we have a pleasing account of Dr. Chalmers in his domestic life and in his study at this period of his career: "When we entered the dining-room for tea, my eye lighted on a table literally covered with letters, the accumulation of a few days. (This even before the introduction of the penny post.) It was Dr. Chalmers' practice at this time to reply to his correspondents, whenever it was practicable for him to do so, in course of post. In his answers he generally confined himself to the matter immediately in hand, waiving prefaces, and getting at once *in medias res*. In this way, although, perhaps, no man in Britain had a more ex-

tensive and multifarious correspondence, he succeeded
in never falling behind with his answers. . . . Dr.
Chalmers devoted at least five hours each day to study
—I use the word in its proper sense; he was thus occupied partly before breakfast, and thereafter till one or two
o'clock in reading and composition . . . . It being
midsummer when I first resided under his roof, he generally relaxed for two hours, taking some favourite walk,
and inviting me to accompany him. The Botanic Garden
was a much-loved resort. He luxuriated among the
plants and flowers of the season, and delighted to examine
minutely the structure and beauties of some humble
production that would have escaped the notice of a less
practised eye. He said to me one day, 'I love to dwell
on the properties of one flower at a time, and fix my
mind on it exclusively. This is a peculiarity of my constitution; I must have concentration of thought on any
given thing, and not be diverted from it.' He dined
generally at half-past four o'clock; and it was Dr. Chalmers' practice to sally forth (as he playfully expressed it)
after dinner, from his house in Windsor Place to St.
John's parish, spending at least two hours, several nights
in the week, among his parishioners. The more advanced
hours of the evening were spent in a less onerous way
—letter-writing, or the literature of the day, or the
society of friends. . . . In no respect did Dr. Chalmers
present a more attractive example of all that is kind and

lovely than in the bosom of his own family. His children were all young, but they were to him objects of
daily and most affectionate interest; he was playful
among them even to occasional romping. When absent
for a few weeks, he printed little letters for their acceptance. Mrs. Chalmers was possessed of talents decidedly
superior, of large and varied information, of warm-
hearted affection, and of enlightened and decided piety.
Dr. Chalmers had unlimited confidence in her discretion." It completes our respect and heightens our
admiration to know that the great orator was such a
good " house father," and one who loved to have children hanging on him, and helped to make a sweet,
domestic interior—

" Embosomed happiness and placid love."

The ministry of Dr. Chalmers in Glasgow, so far as its
fruits appeared, was universally regarded as a grand
success; yet he broke it off somewhat suddenly. He
had shown what could be done for the city poor, but
did not like to have the system which he inaugurated
spoken of as feasible only in his own hands, and thought
it due to his system to stand aside and let it be carried
on by other men. He had preached, as we have seen,
with immense acceptance, and published several volumes
of sermons; but the strain on his mind was very severe,
as he never spoke in the pulpit or on the platform with-

5

out strenuous preparation. Then he grew more and
more dissatisfied with incessant and, as he deemed,
unnecessary inroads made upon his time—an experience
which, as we have indicated, had been unknown in the
quiet incumbency in Fifeshire.   And at the back of his
mind there still lay the old desire to be a University
Professor.   It was not now an ambition for academical
distinction.   He was conscious of a love like that of
Socrates for youthful minds, and a faculty for kindling
and guiding them.   Yet it shocked the preconceptions
of a good many devout persons, when the great Evangelical preacher surrendered his pulpit to accept the
chair of Moral Philosophy in his own University of St.
Andrews.

CHAPTER IV.

(1823—1828.)

DR. CHALMERS regarded the study of Moral Philosophy as the proper gateway to that of Theology; and though the class now committed to him did not fall within the "theological curriculum," yet the fact that all theological students had to pass through it before they could enter the Divinity Hall, gave it in his eyes an important bearing on the type of religious teaching which was to emanate from the University of St. Andrews. To influence in a right direction a considerable proportion of the future ministers of his native land was, in his judgment, a more important function than to fill one pulpit or superintend one parish anywhere. He expressed this view of the matter in an earnest letter of explanation which he wrote to Mr. Wilberforce at the time, and also in a speech delivered at the farewell dinner given to him in Glasgow, and presided over by the Lord Provost. In the latter he spoke highly of the work of the Christian minister, but placed it second to that of one who should " deal in embryo with the Christian ministers of the next generation, and on whose labours in the academic chair is suspended the future welfare of many parishes." This language applied properly to Theological Professors, but Chalmers had resolved to make his class of Moral Philosophy tend in the same direction, and so he proceeded : " I shall regard it as above all Greek and all Roman fame, if the elementary lessons I am called to deliver shall be found to harmonise with the lessons of a sound and scriptural theology; if from the first principles of that earlier stage which I am called to occupy in the course of education, a few young and aspiring disciples shall go on to perfection in the school of Christ."

He began his prelections with very little written preparation, but his mind was full of his subject; and the great reputation which now attended him filled his classroom not only with students, but with amateurs anxious to hear a man so famous. It had been the custom in Scotland to teach Metaphysics in the class of Moral Philosophy; but Chalmers confined himself to the science of Ethics. He dwelt on the essential and unalterable quality of moral distinctions, and discussed theories of virtue. Then he concluded his course with a series of lectures on Natural Theology. His own way of putting it is—that he dealt with (1) "the moralities which reciprocate between man and man on earth; and (2) the moralities which connect earth and heaven." The latter was the division which called forth the best powers of the Professor, being most congenial to his mind. He spoke of it as "the outgoings of Moral Philosophy to the Christian Theology." In later years, the lectures on Natural Theology prepared at St. Andrews were remodelled to form the introduction to Dr. Chalmers' prelections as a Professor of Divinity, and it may be admitted that this is their proper position.

It would be an exaggeration of fact to rank Chalmers among the magnates of philosophy. He might have been a leading Physicist if he had not found a higher vocation; but Metaphysics could not detain his mind; and in Ethics, though a useful, forcible teacher, he has founded no school, and marked no epoch. In every department, however, he was a real thinker, not a repeater of the thoughts of others. As John Stuart Mill has said of him in "Political Economy," "he has always the merit of studying phenomena at first hand, and expressing them in a language of his own which often uncovers aspects of the truth that the received phraseologies only tend to hide."

It should be explained that the Professor of Moral Philosophy at St. Andrews was expected not only to teach Metaphysics, along with Ethics, but also to deliver a few lectures on Political Economy. Dr. Chalmers was not content with this arrangement, for his observations and reflections on the state of city populations had given him a profound conviction of the reach and importance of this science. Accordingly he opened a separate class for Political Economy, using Smith's "Wealth of Nations" as a text-book. These prelections were afterwards re-delivered in Edinburgh, and then thrown into the form of a Treatise on Political Economy, which was published in the year 1832. His concurrence in the main with the views of Malthus regarding the overgrowth of population and its inevitable penalties has been sharply criticised. What we find to be most worthy of note in Chalmers as a Political Economist is the foresight with which he drew out into prominence what all men at last perceive to be a cardinal question— *the condition of the people*—accompanying this with strong pleadings for education and character as essential to economic comfort and welfare. His treatise, indeed, is mainly an effort to prove the limited range of all merely politico-economic expedients apart from the spread of intelligence and righteous principles in the community. It is remarkable to come on a passage like the following from the pen of one brought up, as Chalmers had been, in the ways of old George the Third Toryism: "We cannot bid adieu to our argument without making the strenuous avowal that all our wishes and all our partialities are on the side of the common people. We should rejoice in a larger secondary and a smaller disposable population ; or, which is tantamount to this, in higher wages to the labourers, and lower rents to the landlords." But then he faithfully warns the " common people" that they cannot rise but " by the growth of prudence and principle among themselves." Elevation can only be won for them " by the insensible growth of their own virtue."

Chalmers exerted a sort of fascination over his students. Armed with a quiet dignity which no one might invade, he was at the same time so accessible, and so considerate, and withal so free of all starch and affectation, that he drew their love as well as their admiration ; and on many of them he made an impression that shaped their character and moulded their life-long career. Dr. Lindsay Alexander may be cited as a notable instance, and his testimony, publicly rendered after the lapse of half a century, is in these words : " He brought the minds of the students into intimate contact with his own, communicated to them impulses from his own inherent energy, and succeeded in lodging in their minds great truths and principles with a force which incorporated them with their entire inner nature, never again to be eradicated."

One direction in which he exerted a very marked influence was quite new to students at St. Andrews. Ever since the "great change" which had passed on him at Kilmany, Dr. Chalmers had been warm and steadfast in his support of such missionary enterprises as were then going forward. We have noticed his interest in the Moravian, Baptist, and London Missionary Societies. He felt as cordially toward the Church (of England) Missionary Society, and longed to see his own Church take her due share in such honourable work. Soon after his settlement in St. Andrews, he found a small association already formed there to promote Foreign Missions, and, on invitation, at once accepted the Presidency. Extraordinary interest thereupon attached to the monthly meetings, at which Professor Chalmers was wont to convey missionary intelligence to the members and their friends. His custom was to take the various Missionary Societies in rotation, giving an evening to each, and sketching its leading characteristics as well as describing its work. On such occasions the Town Hall was crowded with auditors, and it must have seemed to the citizens, long accustomed to the indifference of Moderatism to the missionary cause, that a new epoch indeed had come. The students were conscious of a warmer religious atmosphere, and some caught the flame of a Christian self-devotion. It is a fact ever to be remembered that it was Chalmers who in this way fostered the missionary zeal of Alexander Duff, then a student in St. Andrews, afterwards the distinguished missionary of the Church of Scotland,

and the Free Church of Scotland in Calcutta, and one of the "chiefest" modern apostles to the Gentiles. Other men of honoured name in missionary annals, as Nesbitt, Mackay, and Ewart, also went to India mainly from the impulse which they had received under the instruction and appeals of their beloved Professor, the President of the little Missionary Association at St. Andrews.

At the same time the strong bent towards Home Missions which had characterised Dr. Chalmers at Glasgow did not desert him in the quiet University town. His zeal in that direction was no mere fancy that might be dropped, but rested on a profound conviction of his brain and of his heart, from which he never swerved. Indeed, Chalmers was the very opposite of a fickle and impulsive man. He was one of the most consistent and persistent of mankind. He thought slowly and exhaustively before he expressed or committed himself; but once his mind was formed, and he felt it his duty to yield himself to the promotion of any public cause or object, he did so in a grand whole-souled manner, and never wavered. At St. Andrews there were no "masses" to be dealt with such as even at that period tasked all the energies of philanthropy in Glasgow; but he who loves to preach the gospel to the poor will nowhere be at a loss for a sphere of usefulness. Dr. Chalmers found that sphere in the district of St. Andrews near his own house. Proceeding, as his manner was, on a definite plan, he mapped out the district, visited all the poor families, and conducted a Sunday evening class at his residence. The result of this admirable example was that many of the students began to teach Sunday classes in the poorer parts of the town, and the whole community was pervaded by a religious activity unknown to St. Andrews for several generations.

Among the many applications for sermons which the wide reputation of Dr. Chalmers now brought upon him came one from Stockport, to take the anniversary service for the benefit of the large United Sunday-school in that Lancashire town; and just because it was to aid and encourage a Sunday-school the request was assented to. The school in question then was, and still is, one of the sights of Stockport. It is held in a large building of ungainly appearance, not unlike a factory, and attended by about two thousand children, and a proportionate force of volunteer teachers, without regard to religious denomination. On the occasion of the anniversary, which is depended on to produce a large collection for the yearly expenses of the work, it was, and still is, the custom to have an unusually attractive musical service, along with a sermon by some eminent preacher. It is very amusing to read of the horror with which Dr. Chalmers, on going to fulfil his appointment, regarded what he called "the quackish advertisement," and found himself committed to a sort of partnership with an orchestra. " They have got the sermon into the newspaper, and on reading the advertisement I was well-nigh overset by the style of it. They are going to have a grand musical concert along with the sermon, to which the best amateurs and performers of the neighbourhood are to lend their services. This is all put down in their gaudy manifesto. . . . I asked Mr. Grant if I might take the paper with me for the amusement of my Scottish friends. He asked if I disliked music. I said that I liked music, but disliked all charlatanerie. Thus far I went." On the Sunday the Doctor gave the managers his view of the matter in terms more plain than pleasant, but he fulfilled his promise to them and secured the big collection. "Will you believe it? An orchestra of at least a hundred people, three rows of female singers, many professional male singers, a number of amateurs ; and I now offer you a list of the instruments, so far as I have been able to ascertain them: One pair bass drums, two trumpets, bassoon, organ, serpents, violins without number, violoncellos, bass viols, flutes, hautboys. I stopped in the minister's room till it was over. Went to the pulpit, prayed, preached, retired during the time of the collection, and again prayed. Before I left my private room they fell to again with most tremendous fury." Of course the absence of all instrumental accompaniment, and of all anthem singing, to which Dr. Chalmers had been accustomed in Scottish services, gave emphasis to his amazement at the style of the Stockport anniversary.

Throughout the five years spent at St. Andrews, the journal from which we have already made a few quotations was regularly kept. It is touching to see how the good man took himself to task for every little outbreak of his native impetuosity, and marked the rise and fall of devotional feeling in his breast. He mentions his course of reading, which was at this period chosen principally from among such evangelical writers as Owen, Howe, Romaine, and Leighton. He speaks of taking up Ricardo, and comparing his views with those of Malthus, noting his object in these terms : " To deliver myself in a complete way of my Political Economy, and then to give all my strength to Theology." On a day when he suffered from a slight illness, he mentions one of Sir Walter Scott's tales, and it is the only allusion to them that appears, " In my incapacity for exertion I have begun to read the ' Antiquary.' " It is curious that Chalmers makes no further reference to the brilliant series of the Waverley Novels, or to the poems of Scott, though these were at the time in all men's mouths. He makes an allusion or two to Robert Burns—no more. Cowper he admired, and quoted frequently ; naturally so, for was not " the Bard of Olney " the poet laureate of the evangelical revival ? For Coleridge's writings he had no great relish, though he valued his personal acquaintance with that eminent man. The bewilderment with which he regarded Mr. Coleridge's transcendental talk is thus

expressed in a letter from London, written in the year
1827: "His conversation, which flowed on in a mighty
unremitting strain, is most astonishing, but, I must confess, to me still unintelligible. I caught occasional
glimpses of what he would be at; but mainly he was far
out of all sight and all sympathy. . . . You know that
Irving sits at his feet, and drinks in the inspiration of
every syllable that falls from him. There is a secret, and
to me as yet unintelligible, communion of spirit between
them on the ground of a certain German mysticism and
transcendental lake-poetry which I am not yet up to."
Wordsworth, the great prophet of the "lake poetry,"
was, probably, too vague for Chalmers, though his exquisite descriptions of nature ought to have recommended
him to one so enthusiastic in the enjoyment of scenery;
for Chalmers had an eye for landscape that might have
belonged to a poet or painter, and might often be found
mounting a tower, climbing a hill, or riding outside a
coach for the sake of some "glorious prospect."

The great poets of an earlier time he seems to have
read over with care in his later years. After a complete
perusal of Milton, he remarked that he did not wonder
at the poet's preference of "Paradise Regained" to "Paradise Lost." The power and witchery of Shakespeare he
felt as all intellectual men do, and observed, "I dare say
Shakespeare was the greatest man that ever lived—
greater, perhaps, even than Sir Isaac Newton." His

favourite play was the Midsummer Night's Dream, and we concur with Dr. Bayne in thinking that such a prefer- ence, avowed as it was near the close of his life, is a beautiful and characteristic trait. "After a life of con- tinual effort, of perpetual contact with men and things, after the world had done its worst upon him, both in applause and in censure, he still walked in the aërial gaiety, the many-tinted summer-like beauty, the genial though keen sagacity of the Midsummer Night's Dream. It is a very remarkable circumstance, telling of a gentle- ness of nature, a kind, gleesome humour, an exuberant, unstrained force and freshness of intellect, surely rare among theologians."

Dr. Chalmers, however, was not at any time of his life a great adept in literature or an accomplished critic. We do not look to him for finished estimates of authors, either in prose or verse. His mind worked deliberately and powerfully on the themes and affairs with which it grappled; but he did not read very widely, or take much note of the *belles lettres.*

In the journal we fall on curious phrases. Chalmers always expressed himself with *verve;* sometimes with an emphasis almost laughable; sometimes, too, on the con- fidential page or in private letters, with quaint Scottish terms of speech which he avoided in his published works. So we meet with such expressions as the following: " I was in a bustled and arduous state." " I was a little colded." "I behoved me to make calls." "I feel colded to St. Andrews by the High Church spirit which pervades it." "Mrs. Campbell, of Shawfield, was there, who appears a remarkably wholesome and well-disposed person." "My exercises sadly interrupted this day by the constant visitations of indignancy on the reflection of college matters." "The minister I saw smiling and smirkling." "Mr. Buchanan spoke with an utterance which only played buff upon them." "Much weighted with public difficulties." "Thronged with college and university meetings." "Do thou evangelise the rising talents of our Church!" Those who recollect private conversation with Dr. Chalmers can recall many similar phrases; if not elegant, yet graphic and full of energy. A story is told of his ascending a high hill with a few friends — a feat he always loved to accomplish. When they reached the summit, the Doctor sat down, and looking round with a benign expression, said, "Let us abandon ourselves to miscellaneous emotions!" One must imagine the Fifeshire pronunciation "miscellāwneous." When on a visit to Ireland he expressed a desire to hear the Irish language spoken. An old woman was brought forward, bribed with a sixpence, to talk in the Celtic tongue, and the village doctor was ready to interpret. When she had spoken a short sentence, Chalmers eagerly inquired of the interpreter what it meant. "She says that she wants another sixpence." With quick repugnance

Chalmers answered, "It is too bad; you must really learn to set limits to your unbridled appetency!"

No one expected Dr. Chalmers to remain permanently in the Chair of Moral Philosophy at St. Andrews. He liked the old city by the sea; and even the east wind from the German Ocean suited him. One has described him as walking cheerily along the seashore in half a breeze of biting wind, staff in hand. "'Fine bracing east wind this!' he ejaculated, with that husky, clanging voice of his, like that of a sea bird." But the sphere was too contracted for a man of his capacity. Moreover, he was not happy with his colleagues; and the divergence between them was brought out before the University Commission of the period in a manner which Dr. Chalmers felt to be painful. Accordingly, he gave some consideration to a proposal which was made to him in the year 1827, that he should fill a Chair of Moral Philosophy in the new University of London.

To satisfy his own mind about this matter, Chalmers made a journey, or rather a voyage, to the Metropolis. He had also another object in view—to officiate at the opening of a new church, which was built in Regent Square for the ministry of Edward Irving. It was to be called the National Scotch Church. The following notes of the services on this occasion are found in the journal letter which he wrote to his family:

"*Friday.*—Mr. Irving conducted the preliminary

service in the National Church. There was a prodigious want of tact in the length of his prayer—forty minutes— and altogether it was an hour and a half from the commencement of the service ere I began. . . . The dinner took place at five o'clock, and many speeches. Mr. Irving certainly errs in the outrunning of sympathy."

"*Sunday,* 15*th May* (1827).—The crowd gathered and grew, and the church was filled to an overflow. Lord Bexley still in the place where he was on Friday; Mr. (Sir Robert) Peel was beside him then. Lord Farnham, Lord Mandeville, Mr. Coleridge, and many other notables whom I cannot recollect among my hearers. Coleridge I saw in the vestry both before and after service; he was very complimentary. Walked towards Swallow Street, where I was to preach in the afternoon."

Some of the notes on the following days are interesting :

"*Monday.*—Breakfasted with Strachan (afterwards Bishop of Toronto). Duncan there, and Mr. (Sir) James Stephen, a very literary man, and high in office. Dr. S., Mr. D., and I went forth after breakfast; in the first place, to the courts at Westminster Hall, where I was much interested by the aspect of the various judges, who looked very picturesque; then towards Covent Garden, where Cobbett and Hunt were to address the people on politics. . . . I was under the necessity of going to dine at Mr. Frere's, at two. He is the person to whom Mr. Irving dedicates his book on 'Prophecy.'"

" *Tuesday*.—Hired a chaise for the day, and made fifteen calls. Crossed the Thames at Waterloo Bridge, where I called on Lady Radstock; they were full of kindness. Visited the Bishop of Lichfield and Coventry (formerly Gloucester), where I dined. All was cordiality."

At the House of Commons he mentions conversations with Mr. (Lord) Macaulay, who was not then in Parliament, with "Mr. Peel" and "Mr. Brougham."

On this visit to London, Dr. Chalmers evidently felt serious misgivings about Irving's career.

" *Saturday*, 19*th*.—Mr. Gordon informed me that yesternight Mr. Irving preached on his 'Prophecies' at Hackney Chapel for two hours and a half, and though very powerful, yet the people were dropping away, when he (Mr. I.) addressed them on the subject of their leaving him. I really fear that his 'Prophecies' and the excessive length and weariness of his services may unship him altogether, and I mean to write him seriously upon this subject."

The biographer of Edward Irving has cast some reproach on Chalmers for not having shielded his former assistant when arraigned before the Church Courts on a charge of erroneous teaching regarding the human nature of Christ; and we confess that we should have been better pleased if he had uttered a generous plea in behalf of his friend, even though he could not have saved him from the sentence which impended. But it is only fair to remember that Chalmers never could or would advance a plea which he could not found on an argument that satisfied his understanding, and he did not know what to say in defence of Irving. To his practical mind, with its hard matter-of-factness within " the fiery ring of its intensity," the high-flown speculations of Mr. Irving were peculiarly unwelcome; and that singular man's preference for "ideas looming through the mist," and his ecstasy over the recovered gifts of tongues and healing, seemed indications of an unhealthy brain.

On Mr. Irving's visit to Scotland in the year 1828, Dr. Chalmers heard him in Edinburgh, and made the following note in his journal :

" I have no hesitation in saying that it is quite awful. There is power and richness, and gleams of exquisite beauty, but withal a mysticism and an extreme allegorisation, which I am sure must be pernicious to the general cause. . . . He sent me a letter which he had written to the king against the repeal of the Test and Corporation Acts, and begged that I would read every word of it before I spoke. I did so, and found it unsatisfactory and obscure, but not half so much so as his sermon of this evening."

It is convenient to give here Dr. Chalmers' account of his last interview with Edward Irving, though we anticipate a little, for it occurred in the autumn of 1830. Chalmers was in London :

" Had a very interesting call from Mr. Irving between one and two (in the morning, apparently!) while I was in bed. He stopped two hours, wherein he gave me his expositions ; and I gave at greater length and liberty than I had ever done before my advice and my views. We parted from each other with great cordiality, after a prayer which he himself offered and delivered with great pathos and piety."

The visit of Dr. Chalmers to London in 1827 had for himself no result. The proposal in regard to the London University was not ripe, and it came to nothing. The removal of the professor from St. Andrews, which soon followed, was not to London, but to Edinburgh. Better so ; for Chalmers, while not at all narrow or prejudiced, was a Scotchman out and out in mind, heart, and tongue ; and while Englishmen showed him great kindness and deference, his own countrymen understood him best. His way of blending argument and emotion,.. his combination of strong common-sense with fervent religious conviction, exactly suited them. So it was, on the whole, well that, from this date to the end of his career, the capital of Scotland was the place of residence of her most illustrious divine.

CHAPTER V.

THE Chair of Divinity in the University of Edinburgh is perhaps the most influential and distinguished position that a Scottish clergyman can occupy. The appointment in the days of which we write lay in the hands of the Magistrates and Town Council; and by a unanimous vote it was offered to Dr. Chalmers in the year 1827. He entered on the duties of the office in the following year. Simeon of Cambridge spoke of this as "of vast importance to the interests of religion. Dr. Chalmers," he said, "has been an instrument for diffusing a liberal and candid spirit in Scotland."

From the first day his occupation of the chair was marked by brilliant success, and his class-room was crowded, not with regular students of Divinity only, but also with intelligent citizens who loved the theme and admired the genius of the teacher. In fact, he was now in a position which, more than any that he had yet filled, enabled him to make use of all his powers and all his acquirements. His studies in Natural Science, Political Economy, and Moral Philosophy could be made tributary to his prelections in the Chair of Divinity, the more so that he gave prominence in the opening of his course to Natural Theology and the Evidences of Christianity; while his practical experience as a preacher and pastor qualified him to give hints and counsels to students that would have fallen with little effect from a mere theorist, and the deep religious persuasion which now possessed him had far more scope for influence on others in a Theological Chair than it would have had in any other academical post which he could possibly have held.

Dr. Chalmers had no new theology to teach. His convictions were in harmony with that Westminster Confession of Faith, which, though mainly the product of English Puritans, has become the symbol, all the world over, of Scottish Presbytery. In his later years he often expressed a distaste for the extreme definiteness of such documents, and desired more width and more simplicity; but not because he diverged from the hereditary evangelical doctrines of his Church and country. Indeed, the tenet which he taught with the greatest emphasis was that truth of free salvation by the grace of God through faith in Christ which had made a new man of him at Kilmany, and had been the theme of many a stirring address from his pulpit in Glasgow. Some, however, thought that he simplified too much the nature of that faith through which the gratuitous salvation is received.

Not disposed to question the usual evangelical doctrines on any properly theological grounds, Chalmers was all the less disposed to doubt them on any ground of scriptural exegesis. He never was an exegete. The minute linguistic knowledge and criticism which are required for acute grammatical interpretation of the Bible was not in his line, though his posthumous volumes of Readings show with what regularity and piety he perused the English Bible for his own guidance and comfort, and his "Lectures on the Epistle to the Romans" furnish a good specimen of popular exposition.

In all that Chalmers said and did, however, there was a strong individualism. The familiar, popular theology issued from him in his own way, and with a propelling force all his own. After a short trial he laid aside the old manner of the Swiss and Dutch divines which the Scotch had been wont to follow, and which began with the doctrine of God and the Holy Trinity; he paid no heed to the English fashion of following the course of "the Apostles' Creed;" but blocked out a new method for himself, beginning with man's moral condition as actually seen and known, and then tracing the provision which has been made for man's restoration to righteousness and to God. Theologians will not admit either the superiority or the sufficiency of the method. It is the arrangement of a preacher rather than of a scientific and systematic divine. But it suited the mental habits of Dr. Chalmers to pivot himself on actual and fully verified fact, such as that of human sinfulness, and it enabled him to approach the Christian faith, as he loved to do, through the gate of ethics, postponing the consideration of "higher and transcendental themes." As he put it in characteristic phrase, it made "the order of our theoretical to quadrate with the order of our practical Christianity." "The doctrine of man's moral character should occupy the first place, and the doctrine of God's mysterious constitution the last place, in the argumentations of our science."

The fact is that the intellect of Chalmers could work only in its own way. He was far too prudent a man to innovate in so grave a matter from mere fancy or self-will. He has told how much he hesitated to "contravene the order of every system and every text-book in theology that we are yet acquainted with, or propose to deliver the lessons of the science by a different succession of topics from that in which Calvin and Turretin, Pictetus and Vitringa have delivered them." The mention of these four masters in theology shows that Chalmers looked back mainly, if not exclusively, to the Reformed divines of the Continent—the Swiss and Dutch systematisers. To Lutheran, mediæval, and patristic writers he

paid but little heed. An acute critic among his colleagues at a later period observed that Chalmers was "a
theologist" rather than a theologian. His erudition was
sufficient for his purpose, but, tried by modern standards,
it certainly was not extensive. Many books would have
cumbered him. And the German scholarship which
now affects religious thought so powerfully had hardly
reached Scotland in the time of Chalmers, so that he
could content himself with a range of reading far more
limited than divines of the present day are compelled to
undertake. In discussing the evidences of Christianity
and the authenticity of the New Testament writings, he
told his students what Leland and Lardner had advanced,
and how Paley had reasoned. When the time came to
speak of Biblical criticism he used a compend of
Horne's voluminous work as a text-book; and though, as
we have said, no critic himself, he fully recognised the
importance of the study, urged the students to a familiar
acquaintance with the original text of the Bible, both
Hebrew and Greek, and expressed the hope that some
of them at least would grow to be good critics and philo-
logists. He discoursed admirably on the relation of
criticism to Divinity. "Theology without criticism is
just as airy and unsupported a nothing as were a philosophy without facts; and, on the other hand, without a
systematic Divinity, it is just as confused and chaotic a
jumble as were an undigested medley of facts without a

philosophy." But his own favourite occupation certainly
did not lie " in the ponderous and recondite scholarship
of those mighty tomes which, in the shapes of Polyglots,
and Prolegomena, and Thesauruses, lie piled in vast and
venerable products on the least frequented shelves of our
public libraries."

His great masters whom he was never weary of extol-
ling were Bishop Butler and President Jonathan Edwards.
The former was his chief guide in ethics, and all that
belongs to the vindication of Christianity. "I have
derived," wrote Dr. Chalmers, " greater aid from the
views and reasonings of Bishop Butler than I have been
able to find besides in the whole range of our existant
authorship." The latter was the teacher whom he most
fully trusted on arduous doctrines like predestination,
original sin, and justification. He appealed fervently to
his class to " copy the virtues and imbibe the theology of
Edwards."

Dr. Chalmers did not disdain the guidance of writers
of a rank considerably below that of Butler and Edwards.
He used as a text-book the judicious but commonplace,
and now almost forgotten, lectures of Dr. Hill, of St.
Andrews, generously avowing some degree of pride in
that work, "as having issued from my own university,
and as being executed by the hand of my first master in
the science." But whatever the assistance which Chalmers took from manuals and text-books, no one who

heard him could ever feel as though he were under a mere theological drill-master. The mind of the Professor, whether he lectured independently or commented on the deliverances of another, worked steadily and powerfully through the subject, and poured arguments and illustrations on the class till every one who had any intellectual or spiritual apprehension was conscious of being before a true "master in Israel." Then, as one troop of students after another passed under this influence, and not only told but showed what Chalmers had been to them, all Scotland knew that a notable divine sat in the chair of Rollock.

The "Institutes of Theology," published in two volumes after the author's death, give the best results of his thinking on theology both natural and revealed. It is a work which may be all the more recommended to the modern reader, that its style is more condensed and chastened than that of the writer's earlier productions. The arrangement is as follows: There are three books preliminary to the subject-matter. The first of these deals briefly with Ethics and Metaphysics; the second with Natural Theology; and the third with Evidences of Christianity. Then comes "the subject-matter of Christianity," in three parts. The first treats "of the disease for which the gospel remedy is provided;" the second, of "the nature of the gospel remedy;" and the third, of "the extent of the gospel remedy." This course is rendered more complete by supplementary lectures, and by the annotations or expositions on the class-books. The plans suited the Professor's bent of mind, and so was best for him ; but as a generalisation in the science of Theology it is obviously incomplete. Compare it with that of Dr. Hodge, of Princeton—(1) Theology proper, (2) Anthropology, (3) Soteriology, (4) Eschatology, (5) Ecclesiology. And yet even this is not perfect, for (as Hodge himself has remarked) it assigns no place to Moral Theology, or the direction of the Christian conscience in duty.

Dr. Chalmers was a firm predestinarian. In one of his lectures he describes the horror of Calvinism which he had found in England as more sensitive than rational. "Our northern theology is regarded with a kind of dismay, and this awful predestination is emphatically denounced as far the harshest and most offensive feature which belongs to it. I should have deemed it so too, had it not been for my thorough conviction that it left the offers of mercy, and the calls to righteousness, and all the motives and all the urgencies to a life of virtue on the very footing in which it found them ; and as to any other mischief of the doctrine itself, I think that the best proof upon this and any other topic is an experimental one, whenever we are able to find it. Ere I admit the charge of our doctrine being hostile to the interests of virtue, I must first inquire into the state of our national character

at the time when that doctrine was most zealously pro-
fessed by our people and most faithfully preached in our
pulpits. We know not a broader and a stronger experimental basis on which to try this question than a whole
nation of Calvinists. And if it be true that the theology
of our pulpits is fitted to shed a withering blight on all
the moralities of the human character, what is the explanation which can be offered, if it be found, notwithstanding an influence so baleful, that Scotland, at the time
when that theology most flourished and prevailed, lifted,
throughout all her parishes, so erect a front among the
nations of Christendom—not for the intelligence alone,
but for the worth and practical virtues of her population?"

At the same time, Chalmers could not be a bigot
about this or any dogma. He distinguished between
the truth of a doctrine and its necessity as an article of
faith, either to the Church or to an individual Christian.
Far from looking coldly on non-Calvinists, he pleaded
for agreement with them, remarking, in his characteristic
style, that "movements of divergence" should cease and
a "movement of convergence" begin. He also was
quite aware that, though the tenet of Divine predestination
must not and should not limit offers of mercy or weaken
calls to righteousness, it may be, and has been, so taught
as to produce the benumbing effect of fatalism on the
unhappy hearers. Therefore he earnestly warned his
students against injuring the gospel " by a misunderstood

and misapplied Calvinism." He never let himself or them forget that they were in training for the ministry of the Word ; and it was quite a feature in his course that, after expounding some arduous doctrine, he gave a lecture on the way in which it should be taught to the people, thus utilising his own experience in the pulpit and the pastoral care. When he had completed his instruction on " the disease for which the gospel remedy is provided " he added a lecture on "the practical and pulpit treatment of this subject." When he had descanted on the Atonement, he at once addressed the class "on the preaching of Christ crucified as the great vehicle for the lessons of a full and free gospel." And at the end of his second-part he lectured " on the preaching of good works and of all virtue." One of the supplementary lectures has this title : "On the distinction between the mode in which Theology should be learned at the Hall and the mode in which it should be taught from the pulpit "—a theme which would not have occurred to any mere theological pedant ! But Chalmers knew what might, could, and should be done in a pulpit, and what might, could, and should not.

The views of Dr. Chalmers on Church government were very mild. He was a Presbyterian, but allowed that Independency might be lawful, and that Episcopacy was lawful. Enough that neither of these forms was obligatory. "Instead of being decisively settled in Scripture,

Church government has been left very much to the discretion of Christian men." He attached far more importance to the independence of the Church than to its form of polity, and so early as the year 1831 wrote for his class words which contain all that he afterwards contended for in a long and momentous controversy. "In Scotland the Church permits no interference whatever by the civil power in things ecclesiastical. Her doctrine, her discipline, her modes of worship are her own."

We find no evidence that the mind of Chalmers looked at the growth of doctrinal ideas along the line of historical perspective, or examined with care that dispensational development of truth and privilege which has so much interest for present-day students. Neither did he make much of prophecy. He listened patiently to Mr. Irving, and to wiser men who had made a special study of the visions and predictions in Scripture ; but their solutions were too problematical to satisfy a mind like his. When he alludes to the subject it is always with some hesitation and reserve. Yet it seems certain that he leaned decidedly towards those Millenarian or Premillenarian views which have been generally discredited by the Scottish clergy. In proof of this we may cite two or three extracts from letters of his which have been published :

To Mrs. Paul. (St. Andrews, 20th Oct., 1827.) "I

am now reading in ordinary the Book of Isaiah, and derive occasional aid from M'Culloch's Lectures. He is not a Millenarian, which I am now very much inclined to be."

To Rev. C. Bridges. (Burntisland, 12th April, 1836.) " I find that Mr. Bickersteth is decided in opinion of Christ's personal reign, and I am very far from being decided against it. But I have not yet got beyond Mede upon this question, who certainly left it indeterminate, though I am far more confident than I wont to be that there is to be a coming of Christ which is to precede the Millennium."

To Rev. Horatius Bonar. (Edinburgh, 9th Jan., 1847.) " I approximate much nearer to your prophetical views than I did in my younger days."

No one ever proclaimed the insufficiency of a mere *head religion*, or dry orthodoxy, more than Chalmers did to his theological class. He warned the students that their having mastered the propositions of Christianity might avail them as little in real religion as " having mastered the propositions in conic sections." " There are examples innumerable in the history of the Church—sound and erudite theologians, champions, redoubted champions, of leading articles in the evangelical system, yet without one particle in their hearts of the spirit or unction of evangelical piety." He therefore exhorted the young candidates for the ministry not to think it enough to make

attainments in didactic theology, and not to give themselves up to the keenness of controversial theology
(*theologia elenctica*), but to be vital Christians, spiritual
men, adding to the acquisition of the truth "the experience of its effects in transforming the character and
hastening forward the preparations of eternity."   He had
in his memory the years when he had himself, though
minister of a parish, been a stranger to the power of the
truth ; and he did not hide it from the young men before
him that he desired them above all things to be from
the outset living and enlightened Christians, humble,
devout, and "serious in a serious cause."

CHAPTER VI.

VISITS TO ENGLAND AND TO FRANCE.

WE have seen that Dr. Chalmers was a kindly, companionable man, who visited his friends, and had a keen pleasure in intelligent conversation. He was without small talk, and did not speak freely unless he was drawn out on some favourite theme. But he always impressed himself on those whom he met in society, or into whose houses he entered, as a man of power and a man of God, while candid and unaffected as a child.

He vastly enjoyed occasional expeditions into England, partly because he was a great lover of quiet scenery, partly because he had relatives and friends on English ground whom he wished to see, but also because he was glad of the opportunity to see influential men and advance cherished projects in the Metropolis, notwithstanding its "insufferable urgency." It will be remembered that his early plan for himself at Kilmany was to regulate his private expenditure so as to have an "occasional jaunt to London." It was a modest ambition, and was gratified far beyond what the young country pastor could have dreamed.

At the period of his life which we have now reached Dr. Chalmers was more than once in London, and in other cities of England; and very interesting accounts of the observations which he made and the impressions he conveyed and received have, happily, been preserved. His reputation as an author, and the *furore* excited by his former appearance in London, gave him access to the very *élite* of the intellectual and religious society of the time; and he was fully recognised as a man of the first class, one of the living powers of his generation. Sir James Mackintosh, Lord Lansdowne, Lord (then Mr.) Brougham, Mr. Coleridge, Dr. Lushington, Mrs. Joanna Baillie, and Sir Robert Inglis were among his appreciative friends. In the splendid philanthropic circle of the Gurneys, the Hoares, and Mrs. Fry he saw with delight that practical demonstration of the power of Christian faith and love for which he had so often pleaded. Mr. J. J. Gurney wrote his reminiscences of Dr. Chalmers at this period. In these there is a description of a visit paid to Mr. Wilberforce, with a graphic account of the senator and the divine in conversation.

"Our morning passed delightfully. Chalmers was,

indeed, comparatively silent, as he often is when many persons are collected, and the stream of conversation flowed between ourselves and the ever lively Wilberforce I have seldom observed a more amusing and pleasing contrast between two great men than between Wilberforce and Chalmers. Chalmers is stout and erect, with a broad countenance, Wilberforce minute and singularly twisted. Chalmers, both in body and mind, moves with a deliberate step; Wilberforce, infirm as he is in his advanced years, flies about with astonishing activity, and while with nimble finger he seizes on everything that adorns or diversifies his path, his mind flits from object to object with unceasing versatility. I often think that particular men bear about with them an analogy to particular animals. Chalmers is like a good-tempered lion, Wilberforce is like a bee. Chalmers can say a pleasant thing now and then, and laugh when he has said it, and he has a strong touch of humour in his countenance; but in general he is *grave*, his thoughts grow to a great size before they are uttered. Wilberforce sparkles with life and wit, and the characteristic of his mind is 'rapid productiveness.' A man might be in Chalmers' company for an hour, especially in a party, without knowing who or what he was, though in the end he would be sure to be detected by some unexpected display of powerful originality. Wilberforce, except when fairly asleep, is never latent. Chalmers knows how to veil himself in a decent cloud, Wilberforce is always in sunshine. Seldom, I believe, has any mind been more strung to a perpetual tune of love and praise. Yet these persons, distinguished as they are from the world at large and from each other, present some admirable points of resemblance. Both of them are broad thinkers and liberal feelers; both of them are arrayed in humility, meekness, and charity; both appear to hold self in little reputation; above all, both love the Lord Jesus Christ and reverently acknowledge him to be their *only Saviour.*"

During one of his visits to London Dr. Chalmers went to Court, as a member of a deputation from the Church of Scotland, charged with an address of congratulation to King William IV. on his accession to the throne. His account of the occasion, given in a letter to one of his daughters, is amusing. " We went in three coaches, and landed at the palace entry about half-past one. Ascended the stair ; passed through a magnificent lobby, between rows of glittering attendants all dressed in gold and scarlet. Ushered into a large ante-room, full of all sorts of company walking about and collecting there for attendance on the levée : military and naval officers in splendid uniforms ; high legal gentlemen with enormous wigs ; ecclesiastics, from archbishops to curates and inferior clergy. Our deputation made a most respectable appearance among them, with our cocked three-cornered hats under our arms, our bands upon our breasts, and our gowns of Geneva upon our backs. Mine did not lap so close as I would have liked, so that I was twice as thick as I should be; and it must have been palpable to every eye at the first glance that I was the greatest man there, and that though I took all care to keep my coat unbuttoned and my gown quite open. However, let not mamma be alarmed, for I made a most respectable appearance, and was treated with the utmost attention. I saw the Archbishop of York in the room, but did not get within speech of him. To make up for this, however, I was introduced to the Archbishop of Canterbury, who was very civil; saw the Bishop of London, with whom I had a good deal of talk, and am to dine on Friday; was made up to by Admiral Sir Philip Durham; and was further introduced, at their request, to Sir John Leach, Master of the Rolls, to Lord Chief Justice Tindall, to the Marquis of Bute, &c. But far the most interesting object there was Talleyrand— whom I could get nobody to introduce me to—splendidly attired as the French Ambassador, attended by some French military officers. I gazed with interest on the old shrivelled face of him, and thought I could see there the lines of deep reflection and lofty talent. His moral physiognomy, however, is a downright blank. He was by far the most important continental personage in the room, and drew all eyes. I was further in conversation with Lord Melville, Mr. Spencer Percival, and Mr. Henry

Drummond. The door to the middle apartment was at length opened for us, when we entered in processional order. The Moderator first, with Drs. Macknight and Cook on each side of him ; I and Dr. Lee side by side followed ; Mr. Paul and Mr. George Sinclair, with their swords and bags, formed the next row ; then Sir John Connel and Sir Henry Jardine ; and last of all, Mr. Pringle, M.P., and Dr. Stewart. We stopped in the middle room—equally crowded with the former, and alike splendid with mirrors, chandeliers, pictures, and gildings of all sorts on the roof and walls—for about ten minutes, when at length the folding-doors to the grand state-room were thrown open. We all made a low bow on our first entry, and the king, seated on the throne at the opposite end, took off his hat, putting it on again. We marched up to the middle of the room and made another low bow, when the king again took off his hat ; we then proceeded to the foot of the throne and all made a third low bow, on which the King again took off his hat. After this the Moderator read his address, which was a little long, and the king bowed repeatedly while it was reading. The Moderator then reached the address to the king upon the throne, who took it from him and gave it to Sir Robert Peel on his left hand, who in his turn gave the king his written reply, which he read very well. After this the Moderator went up to the stool before the throne, leaned his left knee upon it, and kissed the king's hand. We each in our turn did the same thing; the Moderator naming every one of us as we advanced. I went through my kneel and my kiss very comfortably. The king said something to each of us. His first question to me was, 'Do you reside constantly in Edinburgh?' I said, 'Yes, an't please your Majesty.' His next question was, 'How long do you remain in town?' I said, 'Till Monday, an't please your Majesty.' I then descended the steps leading from the foot of the throne to the floor, and fell into my place in the deputation. After we had all been thus introduced, we began to retire in a body just as we had come, bowing all the way with our faces to the king, and so moving backwards, when the king called out, 'Don't go away, gentlemen; I shall leave the throne and the queen will succeed me.' We stopped in the middle of the floor, when the most beautiful living sight I ever beheld burst upon our delighted gaze—the queen with twelve maids of honour, in a perfect spangle of gold and diamonds, entered the room. I am sorry I cannot go over in detail the particulars of their dresses; only that their lofty plumes upon their heads and their long sweeping trains upon the floor had a very magnificent effect. She took her seat on the throne, and we made the same profound obeisances as before, advancing to the foot of the steps that lead to the footstool of the throne. A short address was read to her as before; and her reply was most beautifully given in a rather tremulous voice, and just as low as that I could only hear and no more. We went through the same ceremonial of advancing successively and kissing hands, and then retired with three bows, which the queen returned most gracefully, but with all the simplicity—I had almost said bashfulness—of a timid country girl. She is really a very natural and amiable-looking person."

Seven years later Dr. Chalmers had another day at Court. Queen Victoria had succeeded William, and Chalmers was on two deputations sent with loyal addresses, one from the Church of Scotland, the other from the University of Edinburgh. Of the latter he seems to have been leader, and he describes his performance thus :

" This, being the first of all Queen Victoria's levees, was crowded beyond all example. We had sad squeezing to get into the second room, and thence to the third, or chamber of presence. Got my first view of the Queen on entering the third or last room. A most interesting girlish sensibility to the realities of her situation, with sufficient self-command, but withal simple, timid, tremulous, and agitated, that rendered her to me far more interesting, and awoke a more feeling and fervent loyalty in my heart than could have been done by any other exhibition. Having kissed her hand and passed, and forgetting to give her my University address, wrapped up in a roll, I was proceeding along with it in my hand when I was checked by one of the lords in waiting, and instantly put it into the hands of her Majesty."

The cordiality shown to Dr. Chalmers at this period by the archbishop and by several of the English bishops— not least by Bishop Philpotts, of Exeter—was largely due to his conspicuous defence of National Establishments of Religion. For mere pomp and *prestige* conferred by the State he cared little. It was the utility of the parochial system that he prized. With contempt of Dissenters he had no sympathy whatever. On the contrary, he said publicly at Bristol, in the year 1830: "In connection with an Establishment we wish ever to see an able, vigorous, and flourishing Dissenterism. The services of Dissenters are needed to supplement the deficiencies, and to correct and compensate for the vices, of an Establishment, as far as that Establishment has the misfortune to labour under the evil of a lax and negligent administration, a corrupt and impure patronage. Such wholesome dissent is a purifier, and because a purifier, a strengthener of the Church." It will be observed that here also Chalmers thought of practical work and results only, and gave himself no concern about the validity of "orders" among the Nonconformists. Seeing so vividly the need of Christian teaching and activity, he cared not to stop any one with the inquiry, "Who gave thee authority to speak or to work for

Jesus Christ?" Still he was very firm in the persuasion that the maintenance of a national clergy, with "the frequent parish church—that most beauteous spectacle to a truly Christian heart, because to him the richest in moral associations—was absolutely indispensable to preserve and continue the Christianity of the country. We are ready," he said, "to admit that the working of the apparatus might be made greatly more efficient, but we at the same time contend that, were it taken down, the result would be tantamount to a moral blight on the length and breadth of our land." He went so far in this direction as actually to applaud the Church Establishment in Ireland. Before a Select Committee of the House of Commons he said, in 1830: "I hold the Established Church of Ireland, in spite of all that has been alleged against it, to be our very best machinery for the moral and political regeneration of that country. Were it to be overthrown, I should hold it a death-blow to the best hopes of Ireland." But he added some strong observations on the necessity of using the right of Church patronage well, so as to fill Ireland with "a good Protestant clergy."

Dignitaries of the Church of England were highly pleased to hear this eloquent voice from Scotland lifted up apparently in support of their system and their position. They took no notice of what Chalmers always taught regarding the spiritual autonomy of the Church. Indeed, they could not seriously entertain such a view, being the prelates of a Church which, at all events since the Reformation, has never had any such autonomy or independence, either by statute or by usage. And Chalmers on his part did not sufficiently inquire whether his idea of an Establishment was possible in England, or so much as conceivable by English minds accustomed to a quite different theory of the connection of Church and State. He did not, so far as we can discover, even look at the difficulty presented by a prelatic constitution and a sacerdotal theory of the Christian ministry as contrasted with the representative system of a Presbyterian Church in which the rivalries of clericalism and lay-manism are unknown. But it is only fair to him to remember that he never concealed his ideal of an Established Church as one which, while nationally recognised and honoured, should have an independent jurisdiction in the spiritual province as distinguished from the civil; and that he avowed this to be his understanding of the position of the Church of Scotland. For control of a Church in her spiritual acts and proceedings by the Crown, or by the authority of the State, Chalmers could not say a word. Before his life closed he showed what tremendous emphasis he was prepared to lay on the contrary principle, at least in his own country. But at the time we speak of his mind was full of the advantages which an Establishment gave for the maintenance of

Christian ordinances in some fair proportion to the whole population, and for the Christian oversight of the poor by parochial agency. He therefore acceded to the request of many influential persons, that he should deliver a short course of lectures in the Metropolis on the true theory of a religious Establishment.

Any one who passed through Hanover Square on certain afternoons in the spring of 1838 must have seen a wonderful line of equipages; for the Hanover Square Rooms—changed a few years ago into a club-house— were filled with a most distinguished company. Royalty was there, as represented by the Queen's uncle, the Duke of Cambridge. Peers and peeresses and members of parliament were present in scores. On one afternoon nine bishops made their appearance. They had come to hear Chalmers, who sat while he read his lecture, but none the less held his fastidious audience entranced from the first moment to the last. Occasionally he sprang unconsciously to his feet and delivered a magnificent passage with a power that stirred intense enthusiasm, and in one instance brought the whole assembly to their feet, cheering to the echo.

The lectures were at once published, and had a large sale, eight thousand copies having been circulated in one year. Their title well describes their purport, for in those days title-pages were fairly descriptive, not enigmatic —"Upon the Establishment and Extension of National

Churches, as affording the only adequate Machinery
for the Moral and Christian Instruction of a People."
It is quite possible that arrows may be taken from this
old quiver for use in impending controversy, but we confess that we survey the arguments of Chalmers with a
feeling that, however sound in themselves, they have
fallen out of date. The nation is no longer homo-
geneous in faith and worship. The very desire of such
accordance seems to be fading away; and whether we
like it or no, the time of rival and competing Churches
has come. The problem, therefore, about which
Chalmers was so anxious—"the moral and Christian
instruction of the people"—cannot be committed, unless
in part only, to the "machinery" of which he spoke.
The question now is how to combine the operations of
many Christian agencies; or, where they refuse to be
combined, how to prevent them from hurting, impeding,
or interfering with each other. It certainly taxes the
energies of all to cope with the secularism and wicked-
ness of the age.

Honours were at this period of his life heaped on
Dr. Chalmers. Indeed, we do not remember the name
of any minister of the Church of Scotland since the
Reformation who received so many. We have seen
that in 1815 the University of Glasgow made him
Doctor in Divinity. In 1830 he was appointed one of
his Majesty's Chaplains in Ordinary for Scotland, under

the advice of Sir Robert Peel. In 1832 he was Moderator of the General Assembly of the Church of Scotland. In 1834 he was elected a Fellow of the Royal Society of Edinburgh, and in the following year was chosen to be one of its Vice-Presidents. In 1834 another distinction came to him which he valued very highly—he was elected a corresponding member of the Royal Institute of France. In 1835 he received the degree of Doctor of Laws from the University of Oxford. On this occasion he was the guest of Dr. Burton, the Professor of Divinity at Christ Church, and he mentions with great cordiality his introduction to Mr. Keble.

Those were happy years. The fret and anxiety which came with the great Scotch Church controversy had not yet begun. And the good as well as eloquent man was in the fulness of his powers, with troops of friends and vast opportunities for influencing the minds of others and promoting the objects of Christian utility which he had at heart. Wherever he went he was admired by all, and beloved by those who knew him best. What a happy impression he made on his English friends we may gather from Mr. J. J. Gurney's "Reminiscences." Dr. Chalmers paid him a visit at Earlham, near Norwich, and we have the following notes :—

"*Earlham, 7th Month, 24th,* 1833.—As we were sitting in the drawing-room rather late on the evening of the 18th instant, Dr. Chalmers entered with our friend Charles

Bridges, Vicar of Long Newton, Suffolk, as his companion. Dr. Chalmers is a man peculiarly susceptible of being pleased—looking at objects which surround him through a favourable medium.

"CHAL. 'I have been travelling through Kent, Essex, and Suffolk, and now through Norfolk, the agricultural garden of England. It is a delightful country—varied in its surface and clothed in greenness. As to the *moulding* and *statuary* of the scenery, we excel you in Scotland; but when I look over the fields of your country I seem to be no longer looking through my naked eye, but through an eye-glass tinged with green, which throws a more vivid hue over nature than that to which I am accustomed.'

"On the following morning we conversed on the subject of the great minds with which he had been brought into contact. I asked him who was the most talented person with whom he had associated, especially in power of conversation. He said Robert Hall was the greatest proficient he had known as a converser, and spoke in high terms of his talents and of his preaching. 'But,' said he, 'I think Foster is of a higher order of intellect; he fetches his thoughts from a deeper spring; he is no great talker, and he writes very slowly; but he moves along in a region far above the common intellectual level. I am sorry to say, however, that he is disposed to Radicalism.'

"It is always pleasant to watch the noble expressions of Dr. Chalmers' countenance; but he is often very quiet in a large party. I never saw a man who appeared to be more destitute of vanity, or less alive to any wish to be brilliant.

*　　*　　*　　*　　*

"The more we became familiarised to Dr. Chalmers' company, and observed the remarkable union which he presents of high talent and comprehensive thought with an almost child-like modesty and simplicity, the more we admired him as one example of that Divine workmanship which so much fills his own contemplations. I may also add that the more we became acquainted with his thorough amiability the more we loved him.

"I must not conclude without remarking that our dear and honoured friend is a man of prayer."

A few weeks after the delivery of his lectures at the Hanover Square Rooms, Dr. Chalmers crossed the Channel, and paid his first and only visit to France. In those days trips to Paris were not easy and familiar as now. Chalmers could not speak French; but he had good English friends in Paris who paid him much attention; and he preached in the Taitbout Chapel one of his best sermons, on "God is love," to the delight and even amazement of his audience. He was presented to M. Guizot, and as that statesman "spoke English tolerably," they talked of the "conjunction of the moral and the economical elements" as necessary to the solution of great social problems. Chalmers never wasted time on small topics if he could find a man fit to enter on great matters.

It is pleasant to read the journal which he kept on the continent, and to see how fairly and kindly he looked on new aspects of society. "Much pleased with the beauty and lightness of Paris. . . . How much more leisurely everything moves here than in London!"

"The commonalty all well dressed; and whatever the real profligacy may be, they have all the aspect, expression, and manner of a most moral, orderly, and withal kindly and compassionate people. On our return entered a most singular café, leading to a garden, in the midst of which was a sort of templar erection, making altogether a little Vauxhall, with innumerable parties placed on benches, or ranged about tables in the Parisian style of conviviality. We had fireworks and music, to those passages of which that were most responded to by the auditors, I was wholly insensible. There were at least a thousand people outside, who had the benefit of the exhibition gratis, those inside giving tenpence each. I was much impressed by the decorum of the crowd, their respectable dress, and perfect modesty both of look and manner. I have never in a single instance seen the offensive or indecent obtruded on our notice in this city."

Perhaps if the good Doctor had understood some of
the much-applauded songs, he would not have sat so
complacently in the café garden; but far better than a
suspicious or censorious temper was his genial notice of
the good that he saw, and his frank recognition of the
propriety and courtesy of manner among the Parisians.

Mr. Erskine, of Linlathen, was at this time in the
French capital. Dr. Chalmers had already conceived a
friendship for him, and found that spiritual tone and
helpfulness in him of which many have testified, though
he never accepted what was peculiar to Mr. Erskine in
theology. They agreed to make a short tour together in
the provinces of France, and to pay a visit to the Duc
de Broglie at his château. This visit opened to Dr.
Chalmers a beautiful interior of French culture and piety.
Madame de Broglie was an earnest evangelical believer,
and with her the two Scottish visitors had entire sympathy. With the Duke, Chalmers talked on pauperism,
the French law of succession, taxation on land, and
similar topics. Several years before he had expressed in
his work on Political Economy a very strong opinion that
France, by the abolition of primogeniture, had " entered
on a sure process of decay." He wished for "a splendid
aristocracy in every country, and a gradation of ranks
shelving downwards to the basement of society." With
these ideas he went to France. The Duc de Broglie,
however, showed him that the old nobility of that country

had never spent money on their estates like the same class in Great Britain. They had retired to their country seats in order to economise, and had spent their fortunes in Paris. He also showed that the abolition of primogeniture had not been injurious to families, and that the new land laws had spread comfort, brought land formerly neglected into cultivation, and increased the national wealth. Chalmers was right enough in his prediction that the throne of the citizen king, then reigning, could not be maintained on the new constitution of French society. He described such a king without an aristocracy as " an unsupported Maypole in the midst of a level population." But he frankly admits that the observations which he was able to make on his provincial tour, and the information he had gathered from the Duc de Broglie and others, had modified his judgment of the probable social and financial future of France. " My opinion of the actual state of property in France, and also my views of its eventual, have been made more favourable."

CHAPTER VII.

IN PUBLIC QUESTIONS AND AFFAIRS.

(1829—1843.)

SOON after Dr. Chalmers had taken up his residence in Edinburgh, the question of the political emancipation of Roman Catholics reached the stage of admission within the circle of "practical politics." It became, according to modern phrase, a burning question, and was debated in all parts of the kingdom, on one side with exaggerated expectations, on the other with exaggerated fears. Sir James Mackintosh wrote from London to Dr. Chalmers, urging him to publish his "weighty opinion" on the matter. In reply, though he did not agree to "a special publication on the subject," Chalmers expressed his willingness to take part in a public meeting in favour of the emancipation. "I have never had but one sentiment on the subject of the Catholic disabilities, and it is that the Protestant cause has been laid by them under very heavy disadvantage, and that we shall gain prodigiously from the moment that, by the removal of them, the question between us and our opponents is reduced to a pure contest between truth and error. . . . Nothing has more impeded the progress of sound and scriptural Christianity in Ireland ´than the unseemly alliance between such Christianity on the one hand, and intolerance on the other." Such was by no means the prevailing opinion either in the profession to which Chalmers belonged, or in the political party with which he generally agreed—for, as we have mentioned, he was a Tory, opposed to the Reform Bill of 1832 ; and the warm friends of the Roman Catholic Emancipation were Whigs—a party which Chalmers never would trust. But he formed his own judgment, and obeyed his own conscience, nor could he ever be charged with surrendering to party " what was meant for mankind."

A memorable public meeting was held in Edinburgh in March 1829, in support of the Bill which Wellington and Peel had tardily introduced into Parliament. Dr. Chalmers was on the platform along with the local Whig celebrities, Sir J. W. Moncrieff and Mr. Jeffrey (afterwards known as Lord Moncrieff and Lord Jeffrey); and after they had spoken, he delivered what was perhaps the most eloquent and effective of all his addresses. Looking back from our present experience, on its sanguine anticipations of Protestantism spreading greatly in Ireland so soon as it should be cleared of all appearance of injustice and intolerance, we see that they were far too sanguine. But there was sound sense in such passages as the following :—

"The truth is that these disabilities have hung as a dead weight around the Protestant cause for more than a century. They have enlisted in opposition to it some of the most unconquerable principles of nature; resentment because of injury, and the pride of adherence to a suffering cause. They have transformed the whole nature of the contest, and by so doing they have rooted and given tenfold obstinacy to error. They have given to our side the hateful aspect of tyranny; while in theirs we behold a generous and high-minded resistance to what they deem to be oppression."

"Reason, and Scripture, and Prayer—these compose, or ought to compose, the whole armoury of Protestantism, and it is by them alone that the battles of the faith can be successfully fought. It is since the admission of intolerance, that unseemly associate within our ranks, that the cause of the Reformation has come down from its vantage-ground. We want to be disencumbered of this weight, and restored to our free and proper energies."

Throughout the whole of this speech Dr. Chalmers was extremely animated, and roused his audience to a white heat of enthusiasm. The newspapers of the day called it a "tumult of admiration." We have it on the authority of the late Dean Ramsay, that "our most distinguished

Scottish critic, Lord Jeffrey, gave it as his decided opinion that never had eloquence produced a greater effect upon a popular assembly, and that he could not believe more had ever been done by the oratory of Demosthenes, Cicero, Burke, or Sheridan."

As we have spoken of Dr. Chalmers as a Tory, we are bound to mention that not on the Catholic Emancipation question only, but on the repeal of the Tests and Corporation Act, in 1828, he took the Liberal side with great decision; and his objection to the enfranchisement of the Ten Pound Householders in 1832 was not grounded on any mistrust of "the common people," for whom he had deep respect and sympathy, but arose from a misgiving that the eyes of men were being turned from the real moral foundations of social improvement to a mere political panacea; and also from a fear "lest the Reform Bill should throw the legislative power into the hands of men of business—already full of all kinds of occupation—to the exclusion of men who have leisure for deep study and reflection, and are therefore able to cope with great principles on the various subjects of legislation." This at all events was no mere obtuse resistance to reform and progress.

The questions which chiefly occupied Dr. Chalmers as a Churchman, over and above those which he discussed as a Theological Professor, were two in number. The one concerned the extension, and the other the independence of the Church.

I. *The Extension of the Church.*—The bent of Chalmers, as we have seen, was strongly practical. He could sustain an elevated argument on philosophical and theological abstractions; but his thoughts could not find a terminus in these. He was ever musing on the social, moral, and religious welfare of the people at large, and instituting agencies or advocating measures for the gathering of "the population" locally and systematically under the purifying and elevating power of the gospel. Thus he was unwearied in the cause of church extension and home missions. As early as the year 1817 he had made an appeal for the erection of twenty additional churches to meet the growth of population in Glasgow. It startled the city. The municipal authorities were asked to give twenty, and they gave one—that church of St. John's, of which Chalmers himself took charge. A few years passed, and the same question on a much larger scale took hold of his mind. At the end of the seventeenth century Scotland had between 900 and 1,000 parish churches for a population which was under one million. During the whole of the eighteenth century, and the early part of the nineteenth, only sixty-two churches had been added, while the population had more than doubled itself. So much for the enterprise of the Moderates who predominated during very nearly the whole of that long period. At last the General Assembly appointed a committee on church extension;

but very little was effected till, in the year 1834, Dr. Chalmers was named as chairman, or (as the Scotch say) convener, of the committee, and brought all his energy and influence to bear upon the object. He began by making urgent representations to Government, and to many leading politicians, of the duty of the nation to provide church accommodation for its own increasing numbers. At first some encouragement was given, but in the end there was miserable disappointment. Nothing daunted, however, Dr. Chalmers appealed to the people of Scotland, and soon gained a great success. In the short space of four years he was able to report to the General Assembly of 1838 that nearly 200 new churches had been built, and that £200,000 had been contributed towards the cost. Before he retired from the convenership, in 1841, he had been the means of adding 220 new churches to the Scottish Establishment. To reach this result he had made a tour through a great part of Scotland, addressing public meetings, and speaking at public breakfasts and dinners day after day. It entailed on him great fatigue, but he grudged nothing for a cause he loved so well.

But while these new churches were being built, a course of events was in progress which was soon to separate their great founder from the fruit of his labour. A question was revived which had in former days roused strong and even passionate feeling among the Scottish people, viz., the right of the flock to have the choice of the pastor, or at the least to have protection against the intrusion of a pastor whom they regarded as unsuitable. Out of the agitation of this question rose a greater one, to which Chalmers had always been keenly alive. It was—

II. *The Spiritual Independence of the Church.*—It is not desirable to narrate the development and treatment of this question at length. And it would be inexcusable to refer to the matter with any of that heated feeling which was unavoidable among a people so keen and disputatious as the Scotch while the controversy was being waged, or even when it was recent in the public memory. But without a brief statement an important part of Chalmers' public life cannot be understood.

A system of lay patronage to parochial cures in Scotland was introduced and legalised in the reign of Queen Anne. It was contrary to the wish of the Scottish people, and at various periods caused much discontent, and some secessions from the Church. Again and again unacceptable ministers were forced upon parishes, at the cost of much scandal and irritation. In the year 1834, when the Evangelical party had recovered their long lost preponderance in the Church, the General Assembly passed an Act giving to the majority of male communicants in a parish the power of a negative, or *veto*, on a presentation. The Church did not presume to interfere with the rights conferred on a patron by Act of Parliament, but it expressed its own resolution not to ordain or induct on a bare presentation from the patron, if the majority of the Christian people in the parish declared that such a settlement would be unacceptable or unprofitable to them. The minority in the General Assemblies of that period, commonly called the Moderates—the same as we have already seen chilling the ecclesiastical breath of St. Andrews — objected to this as virtually annulling the statutory rights of patrons. A severe and protracted controversy ensued; public meetings were held in all parts of Scotland ; the Presbyteries and Synods became little battle-fields of party ; and pamphlet followed pamphlet with keen argument and sometimes passionate invective. The one party shouted for the rights of the people ; the other insisted on the rights of patrons, and ridiculed the notion of sheep sitting in judgment on their shepherd. As the *veto* came into operation—though many patrons took care not to irritate the public feeling of parishes, and their presentees were quietly accepted— some cases were disputed, and serious trouble arose. When the Evangelicals were overruled they appealed to the Ecclesiastical Courts. When the Moderates were overruled, they appealed, or they favoured the appeal of patron and presentee, to the Courts of civil jurisdiction. The General Assembly sustained the operation of the *veto*, and enforced its own jurisdiction, going so far as to depose the majority of a Presbytery which had ordained and inducted a vetoed presentee. In so doing, the Church did not deny that there were civil rights and interests connected with the position of parish minister which the patron had a right to confer on his presentee ; and it acknowledged that the Civil Courts might deal with these, and the State might give or withhold them as it thought fit ; but ordination was a spiritual act, and induction an ecclesiastical regulation, which lay entirely within the jurisdiction of the Church, and concerning which the civil power was not competent to give instructions or orders. On the other hand, the Court of Session, in enforcing the civil rights of patrons and presentees, required that the Church should take the usual steps to place them in the enjoyment of those rights; and the House of Lords, on appeal, pronounced the *veto* law of the General Assembly *ultra vires* of that body, and to be treated as null and void.

The Church of Scotland was not prepared to submit in such a matter even to the House of Lords. A cry rose against her—" Obey the law of the land !" The answer substantially was—that this was not a question of " the land," nor a matter to which law made by Parliament and construed by civil judges had any application. English readers must bear in mind that the Church of Scotland always had a quite different constitution from the Church of England. It never acknowledged the royal supremacy in matters ecclesiastical, or took authority for any of its actions from Crown and Parliament. It went into union with the State on the ground of a collateral jurisdiction, not of subordination or submission. No doubt it might be difficult, in cases where both spiritual and civil elements were combined, to assign to each jurisdiction what belonged to it; but it was held sufficient to lay down the broad axiom that spiritual matters are those which require authority from the Lord Jesus Christ according to His Word, and civil are those which require for their regulation nothing more than authority from the supreme civil ruler, which authority, however, is to be honoured as coming from God for the good of the subjects or citizens; and, further, that in the combination and possible complication of these, each Court of jurisdiction must determine its own part of the case, and use its proper means and weapons for carrying out its behests. Thus the State could not commit the mistake of appointing an ordination or regulating a communion, because no officer of the State, though armed with all the "power of the sword," can ordain to office in the Church, or either give or withhold communion; and, on the other hand, the Church could not commit the mistake of determining who shall occupy the manse or draw that stipend under Act of Parliament, because no officer of the Church with ever so much spiritual power or dignity can determine questions of houses, and the right to silver and gold.

It is not necessary at this time of day to discuss the temper or discretion on either side with which the Scottish Ten Years' Conflict (1833—1843) was waged. As collisions between the spiritual and civil authorities multiplied, and were embittered by the circumstance that an influential minority in the Church took all along the side of the State, it became evident that nothing would settle the difficulty but an Act of Parliament which should recognise the people's *veto* as from the side of the State, and so legalise the limitation to this extent of the system of patronage. Dr. Chalmers, who, though not the most active of the Church leaders of the period, was the most influential, spent much of his time in correspondence and interviews with the leaders of both the great parties in the State, and with prominent Members of Parliament, in the hope of bringing about a solution of the whole question which should be respectful to the civil power, and at the same time satisfactory to the Church. He laboured hard to drive his ideas into Viscount Melbourne, the Earl of Aberdeen, Lord John Russell, Lord Brougham, Sir Robert Peel, and Sir James Graham. But Lord Aberdeen, who as a Scotchman and an Elder of the Church knew the subject best, was, unfortunately, opposed to the extension of popular rights; and the Englishmen appealed to never could extricate themselves from the English traditional lines of thought; never could regard it as a feasible or creditable thing, that an

Established Church should exercise a spiritual jurisdiction uncontrolled by the Crown and by the courts of law. An effort was made by the Duke of Argyll (father of the present Duke) to pass a measure through Parliament which would have gone as far as the *veto* law of the Church, and a little farther ; but it proved abortive. To Dr. Chalmers it was peculiarly disappointing to find the Conservative chiefs, Peel, Aberdeen, and Graham, who were then in power, giving heed and sympathy to the Moderate party, and turning away from his advice as from that of some excited fanatic. At last, in the summer of 1840, he shook off the dust of his feet against them, publicly declaring "the blasting of all my fondest hopes for the good and peace of our Church, in my correspondence with public and parliamentary men." In short, the experience which Chalmers had of the Whigs in regard to the extension of the Church of Scotland, he now had of the Conservatives in regard to its spiritual independence. And the issue was vanity and vexation of spirit. In the circumstances he made a rather peculiar *amende* to the Whigs.

"After all, I now feel that I owe an act of justice to the Whigs. I understand justice in the same sense as equity *(æquitas)*, and I am now bound to say that if on the question of Church Endowments I have been grievously disappointed by the one party, on the question of Church Independence I have been as grievously disappointed by the other. Of course I speak on the basis of a very limited induction; but as far as the findings of my own personal observation are concerned, I should say of the former, that they seem to have no great value for a Church Establishment at all; and of the latter, that their great value for a Church Establishment seems to be more for it as an engine of State than as an instrument of Christian usefulness. The difference lies in having no principle, or in having a principle that is wrong. In either way they are equally useless, and may prove equally hurtful to the Church; and though the acknowledgment I now make to the Whigs be a somewhat ludicrous one, if viewed in the character of a peace-offering, I am nevertheless bound to declare that, for aught like Church purposes, I have found the Conservatives to be just as bad as themselves. It is for the Church now to renounce all dependence upon men, and, persevering in the high walk of duty on which she has entered, to prosecute her own objects on her own principles, leaving each party in the State to act as they may."

Negotiations, however, went on; and the shower of pamphlets and speeches ceased not. It is really wonderful that an agreement was not reached, for the parties were at last divided only by the question whether a *veto* without reasons or a *veto* with reasons should be legalised. Dr. Chalmers insisted on the former, arguing that there might be serious objections to a minister which could not very well be specified and proved under a statute, and that, if a presentee were to be rejected at all, it would be more just and more merciful to him to interpose a simple *veto* than to publish his defects in detail to the whole country, and that under an inducement to make the worst of them. On the other side, Lord Aberdeen protested that a *veto* without reasons assigned by the people, and judged by the Presbytery, might be the dictate of mere prejudice or caprice, and ought not to be listened to. Lord Aberdeen had his way. But it is a significant fact that, after a thirty years' trial of the system which he introduced, not only has the *veto* with reasons been given up as a nuisance, but the whole system of patronage in Scotland has been abolished by Parliament under the advice of a Conservative Government. In the Church of Scotland to-day there is popular election of pastors, and the Church Courts have a guarantee of undisturbed jurisdiction in all questions affecting the settlement of parochial ministers. Nor does the Act of Parliament pretend to grant this jurisdiction. It recognises it as inherent in the Church.

But the things which are now seen to be safe and wise were held by the Moderates of Scotland and "the public and parliamentary men" of England to be dangerous and even absurd in the years to which we refer; and

Dr. Chalmers foresaw, quite eighteen months before the event, that the accumulating difficulties would end in a prodigious crash. We hear a good deal at this crisis of Sir George Sinclair, M.P. for Caithness. He was a Conservative of the type of Sir Robert Inglis, devoted to Church and State and the Protestant Constitution. He had been active in bringing Chalmers to London to lecture on " Religious Establishments" at the Hanover Square Rooms; and he was now most anxious to prevent disaster to the Church of Scotland. But we find Chalmers writing to him in September, 1841, in terms that foreshadowed very serious issues :

" I reserve myself for one emergency. Should there be a disruption of the Church, I shall feel it my duty to help forward the operations of a great home mission, which I have no doubt could take full possession of the country in a very few months. And, looking to the Christian interests of Scotland, I believe that more good could be done through such an instrumentality than by an Established Church exposed to such interferences as those of the Court of Session for the last few years."

It is said that when a friend once asked Chalmers what he supposed he had been intended for by nature, he promptly answered, "a military engineer." Perhaps he was right. His mathematical powers, his faculty for seeing the true pivot of a position, his forethought and his skill in organisation, would have served him well in such a capacity. The grace of God led him into a higher warfare, and he certainly was a great moral engineer. But he was more. He was fitted to lead men by his strength of purpose, and his rare power of winning confidence and inspiring enthusiasm. Nor did his practical foresight ever desert him. As a competent leader of an army takes thought for supplies before making a move, so did Chalmers, before venturing on a move which he foresaw to be, in all likelihood, inevitable, take thought for the commissariat of a disestablished clergy. While others were still negotiating and pamphleteering, in November, 1841, he wrote again to Sir George Sinclair: "I have been studying a good deal the economy of our non-Erastian Church when severed from the State and its endowments — an event which I would do much to avert, but which, if inevitable, we ought to be prepared for. I do not participate in your fears of an extinction, even for our most remote parishes. And the noble resolution of the town ministers to share equally with their country brethren, from a common fund raised for the general behoof of the ejected ministers, has greatly brightened my anticipations of a great and glorious result, should the Government cast us off." Here was the suggestion of that great Sustentation Fund, on which the Free Church of Scotland was afterwards launched, and on which her ministry is supported to this day. If there had been a Chalmers to devise in the same manner for the ejected clergy of England in the year 1662, as well as to lead them out in a close phalanx, how different might the history of Nonconformity have been ! How impossible it would have been for an Establishment, however powerful, or a Parliament however bigoted, to treat a Nonconformist Church diffused all over England, but bound together by a common faith, common polity, and common finance, as the desultory Dissenting communities were treated for nearly two centuries !

Sir George Sinclair, regarding with repugnance that conclusion to which Dr. Chalmers not obscurely pointed, seems to have reproached him with inconsistency, referring to his former eloquent advocacy of the union of Church and State. We have already pointed out the qualifications with which Chalmers had accompanied that advocacy in the Hanover Square lectures ; but as this is a point on which he has often been misjudged, we think it well to give his own reply :

"EDINBURGH, *December 4th*, 1841.

"My DEAR SIR GEORGE,— . . . I conclude with noticing as briefly as possible your remarks on my consistency. You speak of my former avowed preference for a National Establishment, reminding me of what you call my own theory. Now, in my London lectures, in my Church Extension addresses, in all my controversies with the Voluntaries, in my numerous

writings for twenty years back, the spiritual independence
of the Church has been ever brought prominently forward as an indispensable part of that theory, and I have
uniformly stated that the least violation of that independence in return for a State endowment was enough
to convert a Church Establishment into a moral
nuisance. It is a little too much that, after the Conservatives had accepted with thankfulness my defence of
National Establishments, they should now propose to
take away from me the benefit of their main vindication;
or think that an advocacy given to a National Church,
solely for the sake of its religious and moral benefits to
the population, should still be continued, after they shall
have converted it from an engine of Christian usefulness
into a mere congeries of offices, by which to uphold the
influence of patrons and subserve the politics or the
views of a worthless partisanship.

"I shall ever regret the necessity of a separation from
the State. But if driven to it by principle, it is a sacrifice which must and ought to be made. I say so, not
in the spirit of menace, or for the purpose of terrifying
bull-headed Toryism out of any of its inveteracies, but
simply to let you know that I for one shall feel it my
duty to draw both on the middle and lower ranks in-
definitely, in order to repair, and I confidently hope to
overpass, the mischief which I fear that our enemies, in
the obstinacy of their miserable blindness, are preparing

for our land.—Ever believe me, my dear Sir George, yours with great esteem and regard,

"THOMAS CHALMERS."

It is often said that the Church of Scotland broke up, or to express it otherwise, was deserted by many of its sons, on a question of the popular election of ministers. But Dr. Chalmers and his coadjutors never admitted this. Not the most extreme man among them would have regarded such a matter as justifying a proceeding so grave in its character and issues. Whether right or wrong in their action, they are at all events entitled to the common justice of having the grounds which they themselves gave for their action recognised and duly weighed. They said that they could not with a good conscience retain their position, if the spiritual independence of the Church were to be invaded or denied. The Claim of Rights which was prepared by the late Mr. Alexander Dunlop, M.P., and which was adopted by the General Assembly of 1842, dealt entirely with the question of the Church's "Co-ordinate Jurisdiction," and the securities for such jurisdiction provided in the Constitution and the Statute Book of Scotland. Dr. Chalmers expressed the opinion that this was the view of the Church's Constitution which ought to be pleaded in England and before Parliament; the principle of the non-intrusion of unacceptable presentees, or the adjustment of Church patronage being rather of a local character, and giving to a great cause " a certain cast of provincial littleness." But here, perhaps, he was mistaken. The English mind seems to have misgivings about large views and sweeping principles, and feels for some reasonable thing to do, neither great nor small—" a step in the right direction," and no more at one time. What it instinctively approves is a compromise between opposing claims, or a medium between decided positions which it calls extremes. The claim of the Church of Scotland was too thorough and uncompromising to have much chance of favour with English public men. Moreover, Mr. Dunlop was correct in his anticipation, that the claim to be independent of the State in things spiritual, though the fundamental matter in the case for the Church, was least of all likely to be appreciated or admitted in England, where the Scottish conception of the relations of Church and State could never make itself known. He wrote to Dr. Chalmers : "I agree with you in the propriety of putting the great question as to our jurisdiction in the forefront of the battle—or, indeed, making it the battle —although my experience leads me to an opposite conclusion from you as to the resistance to be given to it. So far as I have been able to judge of the sentiments and feelings of statesmen, I think their hostility to the Church's independence is far more intense and inveterate than their hostility to the people having a voice." So it soon proved. Sir James Graham pronounced the idea of two co-ordinate authorities "unjust and unreasonable." Lord John Russell could not conceive of its practical realisation. Sir Robert Peel declared it to be anomalous, absurd, impossible.

The British Government and Parliament therefore turned a deaf ear to the representations and complaints of the Church of Scotland. Those who had by their majorities in successive General Assemblies directed the course of the Church saw that this conflict must end. In their view the State, by refusing redress, and allowing interference with the spiritual power of the Church, violated the conditions on which alone they could accept ecclesiastical establishment, and so they prepared to break away, not, as they considered, from their mother Church, but from the Establishment which the State had given, and to which the State now seemed to attach obligations which the Church ought not to undertake. Accordingly, the spring of the year 1843 saw the ecclesiastical life of Scotland in a prodigious turmoil. In November of the previous year a Convocation had been held in Edinburgh, under the presidency of Dr. Chalmers, at which the Evangelical clergy in hundreds pledged themselves "to tender the resignation of their civil advantages which they can no longer hold in consistency with the free and full exercise of their spiritual functions, and to cast themselves on such provision as God in His providence may afford; maintaining still uncompromised the principle of a right scriptural connection between the Church and the State, and solemnly entering their protest against the judgments of which they complain, as in their decided opinion altogether contrary to what has ever hitherto been understood to be the law and constitution of this country." It is the Scotch custom to open Synods and General Assemblies with a sermon. The Convocation of 1842 was so opened by Dr. Chalmers, who cheered the perplexed fathers and brethren by announcing as his text, "Unto the upright there ariseth light in the darkness" (Psa. cxii. 4). Another great service which he rendered was to deliver to the Convocation an address on the support of a disestablished ministry, which showed in a high degree the practical sagacity of his mind, for it sketched out the constitution and operation of that Central Fund, to which we have already seen him pointing in his correspondence with Sir George Sinclair, and which remains to this day one of the best possible monuments of Dr. Chalmers.

Through the months of winter and spring the agitation spread into every corner of Scotland. A last effort for the Church made in the House of Commons by Mr. Fox Maule (afterwards Lord Panmure, and Earl of Dalhousie), with the support of good and able men, proved unsuccessful. It was remarked, however, that the members for Scotland supported Mr. Fox Maule's

motion in the proportion of more than two to one. Home
Rule would have prevented the impending catastrophe ;
but the English members of the House, who could not
understand the case, outvoted the Scottish members who
could and did. There was now a clear issue before all
parties. Dr. Chalmers and his friends were not the
men to resist the courts of law and cling to their emolu-
ments, exclaiming that to punish them for breach of law
would be persecution for conscience' sake. They showed
no bad example of disrespect to judges and tribunals ;
but, to save further trouble, calmly and deliberately with-
drew from a position which had become for men with
their views of duty quite untenable. It was on the day
appointed for the meeting of the General Assembly,
18th May, 1843, that this step was taken by the Evangelical party, or at all events by the more decided portion
of that party.

We do not presume to blame those who did not
follow Dr. Welsh and Dr. Chalmers on that famous day.
It was a difficult time, and good men might see their
duty differently. To ascribe every man's conduct who
did not "go out" to selfishness or fear, would be monstrously unfair. Indeed, it is obvious that it required as
much courage in Dr. Norman McLeod to resist the
enthusiasm of the period, and remain in the Church of
Scotland, in order to heal and raise her up after such a
heavy blow, as it required in Dr. Candlish or Dr.

Guthrie to pass out with flags flying amidst applauding crowds. But the harsh comments and taunts of that period are happily forgotten now.

We do not mean that flags literally waved, but popular admiration swelled around the long procession of ministers and elders who, after laying their protest on the table of the General Assembly, filed out of St. Andrew's Church in Edinburgh, and marched down one of the long straight streets to the great hall prepared for them at Tanfield. Tears of joy flowed at such a spectacle of high-principled fidelity to conscientious convictions of duty. In the van came the sturdy figure and lion-like face of Chalmers; and when the fathers and brethren were gathered into their new hall, surrounded by an ardent multitude that not only filled every corner, but got on the roof to catch a glimpse of the scene through skylight windows, it was Thomas Chalmers who, amidst enthusiastic acclamations, was placed in the chair as Moderator of the First General Assembly of the Free Protesting Church of Scotland.

Even in such a scene, and at such a moment, his conservative instinct did not leave him; for in his opening address, or manifesto, the Moderator took care to announce that the Free Church objected, not to the union of Church and State, but to the subjection of one of them to the other. "Though we quit the Establishment, we go out on the Establishment principle; we quit a vitiated Establishment, but would rejoice in returning to a pure one. To express it otherwise : we are the advocates of a national recognition and national support of religion, and we are not Voluntaries."

Chalmers was too thoughtful a man not to be aware of the grave responsibility involved in the step which he had taken, and which for him and for those around him was really irrevocable. And the whole tone of his mind was opposed to such a disturbance of the ecclesiastical constitution of his country. It came upon him with disappointment of hopes and reversal of cherished plans. He had a reverence for the traditional and hereditary; and this was a setting up of new things with no history. He had no confidence in voluntaryism, except as a useful auxiliary ; and here was the greatest experiment ever made on a voluntary system. And then he was a man who shrank from the sectarian temper of pertinacity for points and crotchets, who loved to cherish a large consciousness of Christian love and life, and longed to gather separated brethren into a comprehensive fellowship; while here was the origination of a new division, accompanied, unfortunately, by a bitterness of feeling which entered into social and family circles, and was sure to mark itself painfully on the history of Scotland for many a year to come. He had no ambition to gratify; he had no revolutionary impulse to follow ; and he was no weak or easy person whom others could lead at their pleasure. He was a large-hearted, pious, patriotic man. It is not possible to account for the course he took with such decision, except on the ground of his overpowering conviction of conscience, that the principle of the liberty of the Church to obey Christ and administer things that are sacred under His authority, without interference from any quarter which is merely civil and non-spiritual, was, in itself and in its issues, of such moment as to justify for its vindication any and every sacrifice. Men may say, if they will, that Chalmers exaggerated the matter to himself and others; that the principle in question was not so much implicated as he supposed it to be; or that, while good in theory, it never can be practically worked out on the lines which he would have sketched. All this is fair matter of debate; but of his integrity of purpose, and splendid loyalty to his conscience, no one will breathe a doubt.

> "Such men are raised to station and command,
> When Providence means mercy to a land.
> He speaks and they appear : to Him they owe
> Skill to direct, and strength to strike the blow ;
> To manage with address, to seize with power
> The crisis of a dark, decisive hour."

CHAPTER VIII.

THE position of Dr. Chalmers was affected by the great ecclesiastical event of 1843, but his occupation was not changed. Surrendering his Professorship in the University of Edinburgh, he became Principal of the new College which the Free Church forthwith instituted, and Primarius Professor of Divinity. He did not live long enough to teach in the handsome building which is now so conspicuous on " the mound," and strikes the eye of every visitor to the Scottish capital, for it was not opened till the year 1850. The professors and students at first met in a " hired house," No. 80, George's Street ; and there, on the ground floor, which was large enough to admit an audience of about two hundred, the now venerable Chalmers delivered his lectures with unabated vigour. Besides the regular students, a considerable body of amateurs attended the class, and every seat was occupied.

One who was a member of the class in the year 1845 has furnished to us the following reminiscences :—

"The buzz of conversation at once ceased when we saw the venerable white head appearing, and the firm form brushing the flying gown through the crowd in the narrow passages. Swiftly the desk was reached, the portfolio opened, and with eyes open towards heaven the old man eloquent was pouring out one of his brief, extraordinary opening prayers. He was not master of great variety in utterance; but intensity and reality were vividly expressed. After prayer, he settled down to preliminary notices. The routine of these was occasionally enlivened by humour. 'I have received,' he said, one day, 'a serious charge against you, gentlemen, of disturbing the excellent occupant of the premises next door, by your pedal demonstrations.' The neighbour was a well-known dentist; and the pedal demonstrations were the plaudits with the feet in which ardent Scotchmen delight. So the professor proceeded—'I must request you, gentlemen, to restrain your enthusiasm, for it is not well to give cause of offence to a gentleman who is so much *in the mouths of the public.*' Of course, there broke out a louder 'pedal demonstration' than ever.

"The lecture, once begun, proceeded with more of the fire allowed in the pulpit than the calmness which usually reigns in academical halls. It was difficult to take notes,

for one often sat fascinated by the professor's delinea-
tions and appeals.   At times he gained a singular velo-
city, and projected eloquent passages upon us.   Sitting,
as I did, near the desk, I discovered that he had slipped
between the pages of his written lecture, occasional
sheets from his printed volumes; and these contained
favourite passages, apt to the topic of the lecture, which
he rushed upon us with flashing eye and foaming lips,
sometimes even leaping to his feet, and ending amidst a
whirlwind of applause.   We all recognised that his lectures were valuable, chiefly for the impulse they gave
us to desire that we might be able, like him, to launch
truth on the ears of men with the momentum of intense
conviction, and very practical concern for their welfare
and well-doing.

" He often counselled us, while stating the central
doctrines of the faith in our future ministry, to speak
very plainly of duty.   He would say, ' If you speak plainly
you will not fail to rouse some conscience.   When I
was at Kilmany I preached one day on honesty, and after
the sermon some of the people asked me how I had
heard of Mr. ——'s fowls having been stolen on Saturday night.   The circumstance was quite unknown to
me.   I happened to preach on the next Sabbath in a
neighbouring parish, and delivered the same sermon.
Curiously enough, there had been some plundering of the
roosts there also, of which I had heard nothing.   But the

rustics persisted in speaking of my discourse as "Mr. Chalmers' *hen* sermon." Make *hen sermons*, gentlemen!' With such sallies he would relieve the usual gravity of the theological class.

" Dr. Chalmers was quite a father in the college, and lived in the respect and affection of all. His colleagues were congenial, and he delighted to praise them. He was quite too generous in recognising talent among the students. He would liken them to one or other of the great theologians of the past. In criticising their prescribed discourses, he would enumerate ' the *memorabilia* of your discourse, Sir,' in a way that raised the student's wonder at the number of good points he had made.

" Such was his paternal feeling for his class that he devoted an hour daily during the college session to conversation with them individually, receiving them in succession in his retiring-room. His homely manner and kindly tone at once put them at their ease in his presence, and the conversation, however brief, never ended without some words on personal religion, and reference to profitable private reading. William Guthrie's 'Trial of a Saving Interest in Christ,' and Owen's works on ' Indwelling Sin ' and 'Spiritual-mindedness,' were especially recommended. Many Irish students had come over to study under Chalmers, and on St. Patrick's Day he received them all to breakfast, and poured out to them his longing desire to see their country pervaded by Scripture readers, and delivered from its priests."

The new organisation of the Free Church, with all its
" schemes " and missions, heavily taxed the energies of
its more prominent men ; but Chalmers confined himself
to a few departments—Education, Church Extension,
and the Sustentation Fund. Wisely so, for there were
younger brethren at hand to conduct the details of business; and he had never been one of those agile men
who can go from one committee-room to another, throw
their minds into every question as it arises, then rush
away to lecture on another subject, or to address a public
meeting. Chalmers loved to settle down on one thing at
a time, and work it out like a mathematical problem.
He was thus an excellent administrator of what he undertook to manage, but could not fly through miscellaneous
business. And the same characteristic belonged to his
public speaking. He would not, or could not, rove or
ramble in his speech, for his mental endeavour was to
demonstrate, and then to drive his demonstration into
other minds. It is told of him that when a co-Presbyter
endeavoured to persuade him to speak at large on some
public question of the day he answered, " Give me the
one main point of the case and I'll work it out ; I cannot scatter myself on a multitude of points."

The Sustentation Fund was not only thought out but
worked out into successful operation by Chalmers. Besides writing vigorous appeals, expositions, and reports,
and presiding over the general committee which was in

charge of the fund, he made a tour in the provinces, and
in town after town met the bands of collectors who
volunteered to gather the monthly offerings for the fund,
patiently explaining to them the nature of their duties, and
animating them to punctuality and zeal.   He also took an
important part in originating the building fund of the Free
Church; and as new houses of prayer in hundreds rose
almost simultaneously in all parts of Scotland, he saw
that for all his disappointment in losing the new churches
which had been added to the Establishment, mainly by
his efforts, he had more than a compensation in this vast
amount of church extension.   In the year 1845, however, Dr. Chalmers retired from public responsibility for
the great central funds of the Free Church.   He was
then sixty-five years of age, and it had always been a
hope cherished by him that after he had passed his
sixtieth year he should enjoy a Sabbatic life of comparative rest.   He found himself at the age of sixty-
three in the midst of the greatest ecclesiastical turmoil
known to Scotland for generations, and deeply involved
in it; but when the sixty-fifth year passed he reckoned
it his "Sabbath afternoon," and he was resolved to escape
from "bustling, various, engrossing work" which he found
to "encroach too much on the higher occupations of
good reading and good thinking."

Yet there was an arduous work into which Dr. Chalmers plunged even in his sixty-fifth year.   From the days

of his ministry in Glasgow his heart had brooded over the condition of the people. In advocating a Church Establishment he had been actuated by no mere love of *prestige* or dignity, but by admiration of the parochial system, as the best fitted, if extended in proportion to the growth of population, to diffuse religious truth and influence through all classes of the community. And now that he and his brethren of the Free Church had deemed it their duty to disestablish themselves, he immediately considered how to work out on the new platform the great practical result of which he never lost sight, and which he called in his characteristic phraseology "the evangelisation of the masses." It soon became evident that the Free Church could, by means of the Sustentation Fund, supply ministration to its adherents all over Scotland, even in the poorest parts of the Highlands and Islands. This in itself was a wonderful achievement. But could it reach the careless crowds in large cities, and do for them what the Church of Scotland, in its unbroken condition, had failed to accomplish? Chalmers resolved to turn some share at all events of the newly-developed Free Church energy in this direction; and with a devotion to the cause that may even be called sublime, entered, at the age of sixty-four, on an arduous experiment, with a view to show by example what can be done for a poor and neglected district by local Christian institutions and agencies. The district which he selected

was called the West Port, in the "old town" of Edinburgh, and it was inhabited at that time by a comparatively degraded and wretched population. He resolved
to try what could be made of it, under God's blessing,
by an active organisation of Christian volunteers for
visiting the houses of the people, and by planting a district church and schools. This he called a territorial
system; for it was ever his custom to attach expressive
designations of his own devising to his ideas and
schemes, and he inclined to terms that have a swelling
sound. So he had called the central fund of the Free
Church one, not for ministerial support, or even suste-
nance, but for *sustentation*, and he signalised the district
round a mission Church as a *territory*.

A fine instance of the ruling passion burning bright
and strong even in declining years! After all the applause and excitement which had attended his public
career, the famous author, admired divine, incomparable
orator, devoted himself with singleness of purpose to an
obscure and almost squalid district of Edinburgh, and
with all the ardour of his spirit prayed and worked to
raise the moral and religious tone of its neglected popu-
lace. He set about the task in the deliberate systematic
fashion which had marked his similar efforts in Glasgow.
His theory had always been that a manageable town
parish should consist of about four hundred families, for
whom a church should be provided with a public school

at low fees. The district in the West Port corresponded to this scale ; and it was divided by Dr. Chalmers into twenty *proportions* (his old Glasgow word revived), each comprising as nearly as possible twenty families. These he allotted to visitors for regular kindly supervision.

The first step, of course, was to survey and explore "the territory." The result was this : Of 411 families, forty-five were found to be attached to some Protestant Church, seventy were Roman Catholics, and 296 had no Church connection whatever. Out of a gross population of 2,000 about 1,500 attended no place of worship.. Of 411 children capable of attending school, 290 were growing up entirely untaught. One-fourth of the inhabitants were paupers receiving outdoor relief, and one-fourth were thieves, professional beggars, and *riff-raff.* It was just what Dr. Chalmers wanted for a crucial experiment. It drew his interest more than the most dignified audience ever had done. So he set his visitors to work in the "wynds and closes" of the West Port, presided regularly at their meetings, heard their reports, entered patiently into their details, and cheered on the assiduous band by his counsels and by the contagion of his own indomitable courage of faith and hope. He prayed over the work with intense yearning of spirit, and was as glad to preach the Word of God to eighty or a hundred poor people in " a loft " as ever he had been to address the crowds that hung on his lips in Glasgow or in London.

From the same pen that has supplied us with reminiscences of Dr. Chalmers in the temporary Free Church College, we have the following regarding the services in the *tan-loft :*

" The locality was obscure and unsavoury. It was said to be the very ' close' in which Burke and Hare had committed their murders.   A loft had been cleared out and seated.   Crowds of admirers used to come and take up the seats so as to incommode the poor for whom they were intended.   The Doctor resented this, and forbade any advertisement of his service.   The sermon which I heard was to children, and a mass of the ragged youths of the neighbourhood sat before the simple desk. Others were present, some of them people of position ; but Chalmers devoted himself entirely to the young.   He used his manuscript, but interjected explanations.   In his earnestness his gold spectacles were now on his nose, now on the Bible, and now in the air.   If the young forgot, I know that some who were older remembered that preaching for many a day."

After two years of such labour, well seconded by his coadjutor, the Rev. W. Tasker, Dr. Chalmers found himself in a position to open a new Free Church for Divine service in the West Port, and to administer the Lord's Supper to 132 communicants, of whom 100 had been gathered to Christ and the Church within that period from the allotted "territory." It was intensely gratify-ing to him. He wrote of it as "the most joyful event" of his life. "God has indeed heard my prayer, and I could now lay. down my head in peace and die."

This may seem to some persons to be rather too much ecstasy over a not very wonderful success. But two things are to be considered:

(1) Such an undertaking was very much of a novelty at that period. Chalmers in this, as in some other respects, was a pioneer. The old school of parochial clergy, among whom he was brought up, went through their routine of duty, and were kind to "their poor," but never dreamed of such operations as Chalmers projected and carried out. The Dissenting ministers attended to their own congregations, and had no time or means at their dis-posal to undertake systematic missions of this descrip-tion. So the joy of Chalmers was not merely that of a Christian heart over sheep that had been lost and were found, but that of a forerunner demonstrating to all around him and all who should come after him the right way of dealing with a problem which was yearly becom-ing more distressing and more formidable—the irreligion and degradation into which masses of urban population are liable to sink.

(2) The West Port system of Chalmers differed alto-

gether from the plan of "special services" which is now
so much in vogue. It ignored everything that can be
called spasmodic. No one ever accused it of being sen-
·sational. Now the special mission preacher stirs up
a district or a congregation for a week or two, then
passes on to other scenes. If judicious men are left
behind to gather in the results much fruit may appear
and continue ; but if not, the converts numbered with
confidence scatter, and to a great extent disappear. One
joins this Church, another joins that, some go back to
folly, others are to be found trying to preach in mission
halls, but adding no strength to any communion, and
subject to no ecclesiastical supervision. In contrast with
this the plan of Dr. Chalmers relies on assiduous
systematic Christian effort within definite limits. It
gathers its results to a centre and stores them up. And
the people whom it rescues from evil are carefully in-
structed and examined before their reception to communion, and thereafter carefully shepherded and taught.
It may seem a much slower method than the other, but
its results are worth waiting for. At the same time there
is no reason why the experiment of "special services"
may not be engrafted to some extent on the territorial
system to break monotony, and quicken the pulse of
Christian enthusiasm.

It may be added here that Dr. Chalmers was strongly
opposed to the giving of doles of money or clothing to

the people in connection with religious services. Kindness was to be shown to the sick and helpless; but the poor should be taught to maintain their self-respect, and gradually to raise themselves by industry and thrift. He would not have clothes distributed among them by the mission visitors, but would encourage them to save the money wasted on strong drink and buy their own dress, like other people.. In this, too, he was remarkably successful; for the West Port congregation, mainly consisting of persons who had been found in extreme poverty, soon showed itself so respectably dressed that onlookers could hardly believe that the church was occupied by the class for whom it was intended.

The relief of the poor was an old and familiar subject of study with Chalmers. He wished to repress, and in course of time extinguish, pauperism. But his counsels were unheeded; and he had the mortification of seeing the Poor Law for Scotland enacted in 1845. There is a passage in his " Horæ Sabbaticæ " which expresses his feelings at this period in terms that every one must admire. It is his meditation on the story of the Tower of Babel. " The passage respecting Babel should not be without an humble and wholesome effect upon my spirit. I have been set on the erection of my Babels—on the establishment of at least two great objects, which, however right in themselves, become the mere idols of a fond and proud imagination, in as far as they are not prosecuted with a feeling of dependence upon God, and a supreme desire after His glory. These two objects are the deliverance of our empire from pauperism, and the establishment of an adequate machinery for the Christian and general instruction of our whole population. I am sure that in the advancement of them I have not taken God enough along with me, and trusted more to my own arguments and combinations among my fellows than to prayers. There has been no confounding of tongues to prevent a common understanding, so indispensable to that co-operation without which there can be no success ; but, without this miracle, my views have been marvellously impeded by a diversity of opinions as great as if it had been brought on by a diversity of language. The barrier in the way of access to other men's minds has been as obstinate and unyielding as if I had spoken to them in foreign speech; and though I cannot resign my convictions, I must now—and surely it is good to be so taught—I must now, under the experimental sense of my own helplessness, acknowledge with all humility, yet with hope in the efficacy of a blessing from on high still in reserve for the day of God's own appointed time—that except the Lord build the house the builders build in vain." It is the grief of prophets and seers from time immemorial, " Who hath believed our report ? " How is it that things so clear to us cannot be discerned by others even when set before them ? But they have not in all cases endured this vexation with such patience and resignation to the will of God as Chalmers evinced. He knew that his cause had been right, and with touching humility blamed himself for its non-success.

In the year 1845 we find the name of Dr. Chalmers among the founders of the Evangelical Alliance. He was unable to attend the conference in Liverpool, from which that important organisation sprang; but he furthered its object by issuing a timely pamphlet. This was the first in a volume of essays on Christian union, published at the instance of the late John Henderson, Esq., which was of great service in preparing the way for the Alliance. In this essay he advocated co-operation among Christians as a step to incorporation. He pleaded that there should be " common enterprises of well-doing," and argued that working together will soonest bring Christians to think together. In the end of the essay he avowed the hope of an ulterior result—" a brilliant perspective " — a comprehensive union by which not only the smaller but the larger differences of the Christian world will at length be harmonised. He foresaw in this vision the technology of dogmatic religion falling into desuetude, and the uproar of controversy stilled. " The doctrines in which many now terminate as if they were the ultimate truths of the record will be found themselves to be sub- ordinate to the one and reigning expression of Heaven's kindness to the world, by which the whole scheme of our redemption is provided.

> " ' I'm apt to think, the man
> That could surround the sum of things, and spy
> The heart of God and secrets of His empire,
> Would speak but love. With him the bright result
> Would change the hue of intermediate scenes,
> And make one thing of all theology.' "

These lines of Gambold, the Moravian, formed a frequent and favourite quotation with Dr. Chalmers. With them he wound up his most finished work, the "Institutes of Theology."

His literary labours at this period were considerable, but not incessant as in former years. He contributed a good many articles to the "North British Review," reverting for this purpose to his old studies in political economy; but review writing was not suited to his mind. Day by day, however, he wrote in small portions those volumes which have been posthumously published as "Daily Scripture Readings" (3 vols.) and "Horæ Sabbaticæ" (2 vols.). They consist of short reflections on passages of Holy Writ, read in order from the year 1841 onwards. Go where he might, Chalmers never omitted the reading of his Scripture portion, and writing down his thoughts upon it; and on Sunday he wrote more at leisure and in a higher devotional strain. These comments and meditations are exactly what they profess to be—written for the author's personal benefit, not for the public eye. They are of no exegetical value, but they illustrate admirably the author's simple and unfeigned piety. He kept beside him five works, which he called his " Biblical Library," and went no farther than these as helps to understand the Scriptures. They were the " Concordance," Kitto's " Pictorial Bible," Poole's " Synopsis," Henry's " Commentary," and Robinson's "Researches in Palestine." With linguistic niceties he never concerned himself. In his " Horæ Sabbaticæ " we are permitted to know the innermost thoughts and feelings of the writer almost too well. It is as though we had hidden ourselves in some recess of his chamber and heard him talking with himself and pleading with his God. As he reads his Bible he constantly lays bare his own heart, acknowledges his faults, pours out his praise and his lowly supplication to his Father in heaven. Chalmers, while in his outer life always labouring and contending for the good of others, not of himself, in his inner life laboured and contended with himself.

> " His warfare is within. There, unfatigued,
> His fervent spirit labours. There he fights,
> And there obtains fresh triumphs o'er himself
> And never-withering wreaths."

In the " Horæ Sabbaticæ " we are struck with his strictness in examining and judging himself. He blames himself for " spiritual cowardice " in not venturing to

speak to individuals about their salvation, and for "sinful
emulations, and the ambition of superiority over others."
When he reads the beatitudes in Matthew v. he notes,
"My most glaring deficiencies are from the virtues of
the fifth and eighth verses"—*i.e.*, meekness and purity
of heart. When, in reading the Gospel of St. Mark, he
came on the parable of the sower for the second time,
he writes, "Let me repeat my own special place and
designation in the parable of the sower. The ground of
my heart is overspread with thorns. Enable me, O God,
to persevere with at least half an hour of devotional
exercise and meditation every day after my siesta, and
may the effect be to loosen and unfix the thorns, and to
eject them from my affections, and make room there for
the establishment and growth of the good seed of the
Word of God." On reading parts of the New Testament
which refer to the Christian temper, Dr. Chalmers in-
variably calls himself severely to account, very conscious
as he was of native impetuosity. Thus on Titus i.: "Oh
that I had better observed the apostolic gentleness which
becomes a teacher and office-bearer in the Church! May
I know what it is to abstain from striving, and to instruct
in meekness. I err sadly in this respect—impatient
of contradiction, wayward, and greatly wanting in the
wisdom of meekness. . . . There are others besides the
Cretans who might well provoke a resentful as well as an
indignant feeling; yet let the sharpness of my rebuke

have nothing more in it than moral indignancy, no personal resentment." And on James v. : "Let me both intercede for others, and crave the intercessions of the faithful for myself. I stand earnestly in need. I have committed many offences ; the good Lord forgive them all !"

The latter days of Chalmers were passed amidst signs of universal respect, and in the bosom of his family, where he always was happy. But he had not many intimate friends. The fact is that under all his frankness and cordiality of spirit there lay a strong reserve, within which hardly any one was admitted but the God before whom his heart was open, and to whom he sought to approve himself as a true servant of Christ. He had his own musings apart, and, after the manner of strong-minded men, conversed chiefly with himself. In his meditations, written June, 1842, in the thick of the ecclesiastical conflict, he notes that he was "intimate with neither of the parties in the Church." And he adds, " I am conversant more with principles than persons. I begin to suspect that the intensity of my own separate pursuit has isolated me from living men ; and there is a want of that amalgamation about me which cements the companionships and closer brotherhoods that obtain in society."

Once more he visited London, in order to give evidence before a committee of the House of Commons, on the question of the refusal of sites for Free Churches

by certain landowners in Scotland.   Before the committee he was subjected to a severe examination by Sir
James Graham, but met his questions with a spirit and
ability that showed no failure of intellectual power.   He
finishes his own account of the examination thus : " And
so we concluded in a state of great exhaustion, yet with
an erect demeanour and visage unabashed."   The only
public appearance which he made was in the pulpit of
the Marylebone Presbyterian Church, on 9th May, 1847.
It was the last occasion of his preaching in London, and
the sermon was that which is the best known of all his
published discourses, on " The Expulsive Power of a New
Affection."   Lord John Russell, Lord   Morpeth, and
other persons of distinction were present.   On the same
afternoon Dr. Chalmers received a visit from the great
Wesleyan leader, Dr. Bunting, for whom he had a great
regard.   His own note is, " Most exquisite interview with
one of the best and wisest of men."   During the week
following he met in society and at the Athenæum some
of the more eminent men of the day, *e.g.*, Dr. Whewell,
Sir Charles Lyall, Isaac Taylor, and the Hon. and Rev.
Baptist Noel.   With Lord Morpeth and Sir   Charles
Trevelyan he conferred on those social and philanthropic
questions which were never far from his thoughts, and
sets them down as " the most interesting people" he had
met in London ; this, no doubt, because they talked of
what interested him.   But he mentions a visit paid to a

man of more mark than any whom we have named—
Thomas Carlyle. " A strong-featured man, and of strong
sense. We were most cordial and coalescing, and he
very complimentary and pleasant. The points on which
I was most interested were his approval of my territorial
system, and his eulogy on direct thinking, to the utter
disparagement of those subjective philosophers who are
constantly thinking upon thinking. We stopped more
than an hour with him."

In the recently published " Reminiscences" Mr. Carlyle
refers to this interview as follows : " Chalmers was himself very beautiful to us during that hour, grave—not
too grave—earnest, cordial face and figure very little
altered, only the head had grown white, and in the eyes
and features you could read something of a serene sad-
ness, as if evening and star-crowned night were coming
on, and the hot noises of the day growing unexpectedly
insignificant to one. We had little thought this would
be the last of Chalmers ; but in a few weeks after he
suddenly died. . . . He was a man of much natural
dignity, ingenuity, honesty, and kind affection, as well as
sound intellect and imagination. A very eminent vivacity
lay in him, which could rise to complete impetuosity
(growing conviction, passionate eloquence, fiery play of
heart and head) all in a kind of *rustic* type, one might
say, though wonderfully true and tender. He had a
burst of genuine fun, too, I have heard, of the same

honest but most plebeian broadly natural character ; his laugh was a hearty, low guffaw ; and his tones in preaching would rise to the piercingly pathetic—no preacher ever went so into one's heart." [1]

From London, Dr. Chalmers went to Brighton, where he preached in the Presbyterian Church, Queen's Road ; then went down to Oxford with Dr. Buckland, and proceeded to the neighbourhood of Bristol on a visit to one of his married sisters. He preached what proved to be his last sermon in the Independent Chapel at Whitfield, and took one of his favourite texts—Isaiah xxvii. 4, 5.

On the following Friday he returned to his home in Edinburgh, and on Sunday morning attended the Free Church at Morningside. He spent the evening with his family in a happy mood, and retired early to rest. "And he was not, for God took him." In the morning his body was found cold and lifeless, death having probably occurred hours before. Apparently he had passed away without a struggle, his countenance bearing no trace of disturbance or suffering, but fixed in majestic repose,

> "Like one who wraps the drapery of his couch
> About him, and lies down to pleasant dreams."

A king of men had passed from the earth ; and through all Christendom there went a wave of tender sorrow. The great Chalmers was dead.

They buried him in the Grange Cemetery at Edin-

[1] Reminiscences of Thomas Carlyle," vol. i.p. 159.

burgh ; and it is said that, besides the long procession of mourners, which included the magistrates of the city in their robes, and the representatives of many public bodies, more than a hundred thousand spectators lined the road over which his honoured dust was drawn to its resting-place. Hugh Miller wrote in the " Witness" newspaper of the following morning : " Never before, in at least the memory of man, did Scotland witness such a funeral. Greatness of the mere extrinsic type can always command a showy pageant ; but mere extrinsic greatness never yet succeeded in purchasing the tears of a people ; and the spectacle of yesterday—in which the trappings of grief, worn not as idle signs, but as the representatives of a real sorrow, were borne by well-nigh half of the population of the metropolis, and blackened the public ways for furlong after furlong, and mile after mile—was such as Scotland has rarely witnessed, and which mere rank or wealth, when at the highest or the fullest, were never yet able to buy. It was a solemn tribute, spontaneously paid to de-parted goodness and greatness by the public mind."

CHAPTER IX.

WHY WORTH REMEMBERING.

WHEN a friend dilated to Dr. Chalmers on the merits of a rising man, the Doctor bluntly put the question, "Sir, is he a man of *wecht?*" It is a good phrase to describe himself. There was nothing flimsy about his mind, but a mass of solid effective quality. And there was nothing morbid. It was a robust, courageous, sunny mind. His influence over his contemporaries it is not difficult to account for. He had simplicity of conception, boldness of initiative, breadth of survey, and firmness of conviction ; and all these, taken along with his rare faculty of communication, could not fail to place him in the front rank of those who shaped the public opinion of his time. Here was a man who could influence not merely crowds of common minds, but the ablest intelligences that came within his range. Mr. Gladstone has written of him as "one of nature's nobles," and has referred to " his rich and glowing eloquence, his warrior grandeur, his unbounded philanthropy, his strength of purpose, his mental integrity, his absorbed and absorbing earnestness; above all, his singular simplicity and detachment from the world."

The mind of Chalmers had the preciseness of a man of science, and the breadth of a statesman; and its powers were nobly used because actuated by the aims and motives of a man of God. His moral nature being sound and generous, while his mental processes were shrewd and deliberate, he found his way to the healthy side of questions, and enforced his conclusions on others not with enthusiasm only, and fervid eloquence, but with strong tenacity of purpose. Dr. Smith, from whom we have quoted a description of the habits of Chalmers in Glasgow, bears testimony to the persistence of his mind : " Many have been under the impression that Dr. Chalmers was more a man of powerful impulses, who achieved wonderful things by fits and starts of burning zeal, than of systematic persevering application of mind. There never was a greater mistake. The main secret of his strength lay in his indomitable resolution to master whatever he undertook. When convinced that it was his duty to address himself to some course of study or of action, he concentrated on that his energies of mind and body, and with indefatigable assiduity completed his work." Dr. Hanna gives similar information as to his habits of study and composition : "The preparatory rumi-

nating or excogitating process was slow, but it was complete. He often gave it as the reason why he did not and
could not take part in the ordinary debates of the General
Assembly, that he had not the faculty which some men
seemed to him to possess, of thinking extempore; nor
could he be so sure of any judgment as to have comfort
in bringing it before the public till he had leisurely weighed
and measured it. He was vehement often in his mode
of expression, but no hasty judgment was ever penned or
publicly spoken by him. 'I have often fancied,' he once
said to me, 'that in one respect I resemble Rosseau, who
says of himself that his processes of thought were slow
but ardent.' A curious and rare combination. In proportion, however, to the slowness with which his conclusions were reached, was the firmness with which they
were rivetted. He has been charged with inconsistencies,
but (putting aside the alteration in his religious sentiments) I am not aware of any one opinion formally expressed or published by him which he ever changed or
retracted. This slow and deliberate habit of thinking
gave him a great advantage when the act of composition
came to be performed. He never had the double task
to do, at once of thinking what he should say, and how
he should say it. The one was over before the other
commenced. He never began to write till, in its subjects,
and the order and proportions of its parts, the map or
outline of the future composition was laid down; and

this was done so distinctly, and as it were authoritatively, that it was seldom violated. When engaged, therefore, in writing, his whole undivided strength was given to the best and most powerful expression of pre-established ideas. So far before him did he see, and so methodically did he ✓ proceed, that he could calculate, for weeks and months beforehand, the rate of his progress, and the day when each separate composition would be finished."

Many men have had as much mental deliberation as is here described, but the wonderful thing in Chalmers is that he combined with it a vigour of imagination which brightened and illustrated all that he said or wrote, and above all a temperament of intensity, a rush and glow as of a prophet. Here lay the great secret of his life influence, his attractiveness, his eloquence, and his sway over men. He was no dainty, finical, self-conscious creature, but an earnest, resolute, impassioned man, to whom truth was great and life was very real. Yet the passion of high purpose or enthusiasm which bore him along never confused his judgment. On one occasion an opponent in the General Assembly remarked on the excitement with which he had spoken. On which he exclaimed in surprise, "*Exceeted*, Sir! *exceeted!* I am as cool as an ✓ algebraic problem." And no doubt it was so. His temperament gave blazing ardour to his speech, but his intellect worked on clear, calm, and undisturbed.

Is Dr. Chalmers remembered as he ought to be? A

generation has arisen which seems to have rather hazy no-
tions about him. His fame cannot wax dim among those
who have any personal recollection of the great men and
stirring questions in the first half of this century; but his
works are now little read, and the idea having gone
abroad that he has not much to teach us either in
philosophy or theology, there is an insufficient sense of
the part which he played in his own generation and the
service which as a pioneer he has rendered to ours. In
Scotland he is remembered and eulogised by the seniors
in all the Churches; so also in Ireland and in the
Colonies. In the United States of America his sermons
and the lectures on the Epistle to the Romans have had
a large sale, and probably still command a considerable
circulation. But comparatively few Englishmen read or
talk of Chalmers.

There can be no doubt that his association in his later
years with a party rather than with the wider circles of
earlier days has had some ill effect on his posthumous
reputation. The Free Church was very proud of him,
and naturally took all the advantage it could from that
clarum et venerabile nomen; but this of course tended to
cool the feeling of others who did not accept the position
or like the temper of the Free Church. This feeling,
originating in Scotland, came into England, where the
admiration of Chalmers had lain in great measure within
the favoured ecclesiastical and university circles. Men who

had raved about his genius so long as he championed the cause of national establishments of religion found out that he had been overrated so soon as he placed his principle of the spiritual jurisdiction above the advantage of union between Church and State, and became the leading spirit in a Free Church.

No one disputes that he was a great orator, one who could rouse, convince, entrance his audience. A countryman, after hearing him, gave it as the supreme evidence of his power that " the people *daur na' hoast* till he let them." Scottish congregations have an inveterate habit of coughing, and often keep up a sort of platoon fire all through the service. Chalmers seems to have had such command over them that they held their breath till he reached his period; then some sighed, and the rest fired their cough as a volley. Then another silence, and another volley to follow. But the oratorical grandeur of Chalmers has more distinguished witnesses, winning as it did spontaneous and glowing tributes from such consummate judges of eloquence as Canning, Jeffery, Cockburn, and Gladstone. The influence, however, of oratory is evanescent. The address may be reported, the sermon published, but the projecting power and kindling ardour of the speaker are gone.

Chalmers was quite a voluminous author—rather too voluminous. The complete edition of his works issued in his lifetime comprises twenty-five volumes. Of these, two are on Natural Theology, two on Christian Evidences, one on Moral Philosophy, two on Political Economy, five on Establishments and the Parochial System, one on Church Extension, two are made up of tracts and essays, and ten are sermons and lectures on Scripture. Besides these there are nine posthumous volumes. The literary bulk is too great, and we have an impression that the "Institutes of Theology" and one volume of the very best of his sermons culled out of the heap would carry down the reputation of Chalmers to posterity with distinction, even though all the rest should be allowed to fall into oblivion.

Some of the out-and-out admirers of our author will not admit that his style is redundant. They say that it is massive, elevated, billowy. Be it so; still it is a style that does not bear to be read so well as to be heard. It is too declamatory, and at times almost turgid, though it is never weak or obscure. The published sermons were well suited both in arrangement and diction for effect in the pulpit, but on that very account may not secure a permanent place in literature. They were always written as in the presence of an imagined congregation, and so have the vividness and palpitation of a spoken style. They are never dull or tame, nor do they fritter away their force in minutiæ; but they have a wonderful amount of iteration, and labour and belabour the point in hand in a way that tires or provokes an intelligent reader. Dr. Chalmers believed in "the *dunderheadedness* of the public," and accordingly drove or beat his main ideas into his hearers with vehement repetition. An audience will bear this from an eminent and eloquent speaker, but readers are apt to grow impatient.

What was good in the style of Chalmers—its dignity, lucidity, and graphic force—came of the largeness, clearness, and momentum of his intellect. What was faulty in it—as its tendency to redundance—came of his writing so much for public speaking, and his eagerness to make his meaning known and felt. He stated and restated his points, and turned them over and over, and insisted on them ; and all this was well under his ardent and even impetuous delivery, but on the printed page it is not so well. Educated persons prefer a style at once more quiet and more terse. And in proof of this observe how the sermons of Newman, Kingsley, and Robertson are admired, while the more diffusely eloquent discourses of Melville and Archer Butler, after being loudly praised, are soon forgotten.

It was a smart saying of Robert Hall, that the mind of Chalmers seemed to "move on hinges, not on wheels. There is incessant motion, but no progress." Hall was more discursive in thought, and in style far more finished. But Chalmers knew what he was about, and secured the effect at which he aimed. He concentrated his force on one important truth at a time, turned it round and round in every light, and would not leave it till he had made full demonstration of it to those who heard him, and pressed it home upon them with all his energy. Till this was accomplished he would not, and could not, pass on to other matters. In this sense it may be admitted that he moved—he was born to move—on hinges, and not on wheels. And it must also be admitted that this, while it may arrest and convince an audience, may not suit so well the quiet examination of students.

We have no intention of claiming for Dr. Chalmers a commanding position in every intellectual pursuit that his energetic spirit touched. It is said that he cannot rank high among philosophers, and we admit it. He might have been a great mathematician if he could have devoted his life to that study which first roused his mental faculties. He might very probably have won distinction as an astronomer, chemist, or geologist if he had followed out his early predilections; and yet his practical and philanthropic turn of mind would in all likelihood have drawn him aside from pure science to its uses, in the adaptation of scientific principles to profitable arts. When he was a young country minister, in the year 1811, he got permission from "the heritors" to lay gaspipes in the new manse of Kilmany, before the introduction of coal gas for domestic use; so confident was he that "gas would succeed," and so desirous to have the manse all ready for the coming improvement.

In the philosophy of abstract and reflective thought much cannot be looked for from a man of many studies and occupied with many affairs. Eminence in such abstruse investigations is attainable by few, and by those only on condition of close and long-continued application. A place may be allowed to Chalmers in the ranks of Scottish philosophers, but scarcely in the front line; and the course which such studies have taken since his death has not increased the value of his writings. He could expound Reid, combat Hume, and discuss Descartes and Leibnitz; but he did not touch the problems of modern Metaphysics and Ontology. He has little to ✓ say to a generation of students who work on Schelling and Hegel, on Hamilton, Mansell, and Spencer, and who puzzle themselves over the conditioned and unconditioned, the *Ego* and the *Non Ego*, the Infinite, the Absolute, and the Incognisable. Of his philosophic writings Isaac Taylor gave the following estimate in the year 1856: "Admirably adapted as they were to effect their immediate purpose—a purpose conservative and confirmatory, as related to the diffuse intellectuality of the times in which they appeared, and well adapted, too, as they still may be, to meet the same order of intellectuality at this time or in any time future, they wholly fail to satisfy the conditions of philosophic discussion, such as it has of late years become."

We do not ascribe to Dr. Chalmers any great importance as an original thinker on theology. He adhered to broad lines, and expatiated in broad spaces of truth, avoiding and evidently mistrusting intricacies and niceties in doctrine. He put familiar thoughts in strong lights. He expounded well, and enforced admirably. Above all, he *enthused* his students, if the term may be allowed. But he has not done much in respect, either of method or of substance of thought, to advance theological science. What must have sounded well when spoken, and reads well as written, if we take it out of the wrappings of the Chalmerian phraseology, really does not amount to much more than what is familiar and commonplace. Wistful hesitating spirits will not find much to help them, and perplexed students will be apt to say that the line is not let down very far into the deep. Moreover, as we have already indicated, there is no recognition of the historical genesis of doctrine, or of its growth in Scripture and in the thoughts of men; and without this the hunger of present-day students of theology cannot be satisfied.

Nevertheless he rendered inestimable service to Christian teaching and life. We are disposed to put this first among his claims to be remembered; and it may be well to set down those claims in order.

1. *Chalmers did much for the Evangelical Revival.* He brought all the force of his mind, and all the influence and reputation which he acquired in many directions, to

the promotion of the Gospel of Christ. At a period when evangelical religion was pooh-poohed as fanaticism in the more cultivated classes of society, and such frigid productions as Blair's Sermons were admired, he stood forward to share the reproach of the more spiritual preachers in England and Scotland, and to correct the prejudice with which they were regarded. A new and powerful voice was heard declaring, in tones that commanded attention and respect, the insufficiency of human righteousness to merit admission into the kingdom of God, and proclaiming after the manner of St. Paul that salvation is not by virtue or by works, but by Divine grace through faith in Christ, in order to virtue and good works. Less celebrated preachers, equally to be honoured for fidelity, were immensely encouraged by having among them a man of such intellectual dimension and force. The tone of the public mind began to change. No one could allege that Chalmers was a fanatic, short-sighted, and of narrow sympathies ; no one could call him a *Mr. Feeble Mind;* and he held and preached with an untiring insistance the freeness and simplicity of the Gospel.

Discredit has often been cast on the evangelical cause by an apparent alliance with intellectual timidity, and a mistrust of science and letters. Chalmers did something to counteract this impression. While he was a devout and child-like believer in the Lord Jesus Christ, he had no fear whatever of the ultimate results either of scientific discovery or of literary research or criticism. He loved scientific pursuits, and the company of scientific men. And though he was no great *littérateur* himself, and could not be called learned, he was all his life long an advocate of high education and erudition. He was one of the first to urge that the standard for matriculation in the Scottish Universities should be raised ; and if he did not himself go far into Biblical literature and criticism, it was not that he either dreaded or despised the study. He strongly commended it to his young theologians in Edinburgh, and expressed a hope that some of them would "rise to be the future Griesbachs and Hugs and Michaelises of Scotland, and so able to cope with the Neologists, and with the infidel and demi-infidel Biblists of Germany."

Besides the imputation of intellectual weakness, the evangelical revival was hindered by a charge of moral negligence. It was said, in some quarters is still said, that a gospel of free and instant salvation is administered and received as a pleasing cordial, a species of soothing syrup for the soul ; and that men, when warned against good works as "deadly doing," allow themselves great laxity of conduct, and, so long as they are spiritually comfortable, care and do little for others. This also Dr. Chalmers in many ways helped to refute. His teaching, while evangelical, was strongly practical. In the pulpit and through the press he constantly urged on believers

the obligation to good works ; and in the missions which
he led among the poor both in Glasgow and in Edinburgh
he showed how evangelical Christians ought to apply
themselves to cure the plagues of society, redress wrongs,
and promote righteousness.

✓ 2. *Chalmers considered the case of the poor.* We have
seen that his advice on pauperism was not followed by
the public authorities, and the demonstration which he
made in Glasgow of a more excellent way than relief by
Poor Law officers was allowed to drop. Nevertheless
his testimony on this subject is not lost, and perhaps has
a good deal yet to effect. Not, indeed, that the relief of
the poor can now be undertaken by the State Establishments of religion, as Chalmers at first desired. The
Established Churches are no longer in such a relation to
the population of Great Britain as to make it fair either
to grant to them or to impose on them the care of the
poor. But with the present system no one is pleased.
This legalised pauperism is monstrously expensive, and ✓
has in it no element of remedy or hope. It may be impossible to replace it by the plan of Chalmers ; but his
argumentation is not on that account superfluous or useless. Who can tell if we may not fall on some modified ✓
system of districts traversed and visited by a volunteer
Christian agency under a combination of Christian
Churches for this very purpose, and so repeat substantially the memorable work of Dr. Chalmers and his

coadjutors in Glasgow? At all events his reasonings and demonstrations remain to help those philanthropists who wish for a closer union of public charity with remedial influences and efforts, and who want to go down to the roots of our prodigious and even disgraceful pauperism, and there apply both prevention and cure.

3. *Chalmers was a master in Christian finance.* He could calculate and systematise, and yet was no mere manipulator of money, but knew how to throw a powerful moral element into the operation of his plans, and so to keep up the tone and character as well as the pecuniary productiveness of Christian giving.

✓   It was no new thing that Christian congregations should pay their own way and support their own pastors without endowments either from pious ancestors or from the State. What was new in the great problem with which Chalmers dealt so successfully in his later years was the self-support of a collective Church on a national scale. The Free Church of Scotland stretched itself all over the country as a sort of parallel Establishment, and claimed to be in spirit and in principle the genuine Church of Scotland. It was therefore out of the question to gather congregations only where they could sustain themselves, and leave rural and remote districts without a Free Church ministry, because the population might be sparse or poor. With all his strong persuasions in favour of a Church being everywhere localised, Dr. Chalmers was especially anxious to

prevent any such partiality. So he devised, as we have ✓
already related, a Central Fund, to be raised by weekly or
monthly offerings gathered from the people of the Free
Church at large, and to be devoted to the common
support of the ministry. His object in this was not only
to guard the honourable independence and self-respect of
individual Pastors, that they might not be the mere paid
officials of this or that congregation, but more especially
to bind the Church together, to impart to it an element
of steadiness, to diffuse through it a consciousness of
brotherhood, and to make it possible to extend it to every,
even the poorest and most distant, parish of Scotland.
In this he succeeded, and may be said to succeed more
and more. The Free Church of Scotland is no mere
Church of the towns, but is everywhere ; and raises a re-
venue for sustentation with as much regularity as Church
or State anywhere can show in obtaining its enforced
resources. The same system, with proper modifications
to meet local circumstances, has been adopted by the
Presbyterian Churches of England and Ireland, and some
of those in the Colonies. In other quarters the plan is
being studied with anxious interest. If such a fund can
save an unendowed National Church from the danger of
breaking to pieces, or having to withdraw its ministry from
poor districts, small villages, and remote parishes, it takes
away one of the chief grounds of that dread and repugnance with which most men who have been bred in an

Established Church naturally regard the prospect of its disestablishment and disendowment.

4. *Chalmers was a great pioneer in Home Mission work of the best kind.* Not merely by eloquent speech, but by yet more eloquent example, he showed how Christian truth and influence may be diffused among the poor and neglected on a strictly localised or territorial system. He is teaching still. There are no more successful organisations for the reclamation of what are roughly described as the lapsed masses, than the Territorial Missions and Churches in Edinburgh, Glasgow, and Dundee; and all of these are on the Chalmerian West-Port model.

In England there is much need to learn in this matter of Dr. Chalmers. There are many district missions and gospel halls in populous cities and towns; and the work is carried on at immense expense, yet with very inadequate and desultory results. No doubt there is a difference between the fields of experiment. In Scotland the working classes have never turned their backs upon the Church, and the lapsed are those who, through penury or vice, have given up church-going habits, but still have lurking at the bottom of their minds a feeling that they ought to wait on God and hear His Word; and the effort of the district visitor is to revive and strengthen this latent feeling. But in English towns large masses of the common people are notoriously estranged from public worship. They have no latent feeling or twinge of

conscience about the matter. Consequently the mission
curates and district visitors have to appeal to lower motives
and coax them to services by doles in winter, by enter-
tainments and tea-parties at the expense of others. Some
are caught in this way; others—and those often the more
manly spirits—turn away because they don't want charity
and condescension; and district churches for the poor
turn out to be very expensive institutions, scarcely able to
continue unless endowed by some rich man, or attached
to some wealthy congregation. Besides these, there are
preaching halls and mission rooms for the working classes,
with theatres thrown open on Sunday evenings to catch
those who cannot even be coaxed into a place of worship.
These efforts are all well meant, and, we trust, have their
reward. But they do not even attempt to develop Church
life—to conserve the fruit of their labour. We venture
to say that what are now wanted are mission premises on
a plain but large scale in the midst of working class
districts—such premises to contain a church or chapel of
considerable size, with a liberal allowance of chambers
great and small, to be used as prayer-rooms, class-rooms,
club-rooms, reading-rooms, and tea-rooms ; and these institutions or premises made centres, each of them, of a
systematic Christian agency within definite limits, with the
view of not only preaching the Gospel, but also supplying
to the people Christian instruction and consolation, and
all those advantages of religious fellowship which are

more needful to the poor and ill-educated than to the rich and those who have abundant access to religious literature. A great deal of preparatory work may be done in preaching halls, but it is only preparatory; and the proper sequel is the Chalmerian plan of the thorough exploration of a manageable district, and the erection and full equipment of a working men's church.

On all these accounts let Thomas Chalmers be remembered. Those who knew him need no such exhortation. Those who were his students or his helpers cry with an air of triumph, " We were with Chalmers," as soldiers who had been in the Peninsula or at Waterloo used to say, " We were with Wellington." Indeed he was, as Tennyson says of the great Duke,

> " Rich in saving common sense,
>   And, as the greatest only are,
>   In his simplicity sublime.

> " To such a name for ages long,
>   To such a name,
>   Preserve a broad approach of fame,
>   And ever-ringing avenues of song."